THE WITCH THE CAT AND JACK

GEOFF SWIFT

©2020 by Geoff Swift

All rights reserved. No part of this publication may be reproduced or transmitted in any form or by any means, electronic or mechanical, including photocopy, recording, or any information storage and retrieval system, without permission, in writing, from the author.

Design and Illustration by Jane Cornwell
www.janecornwell.co.uk

CONTENTS

THE WITCH'S LOST CAT

THE WITCH'S BROKEN BROOM

THE MISSING STAR

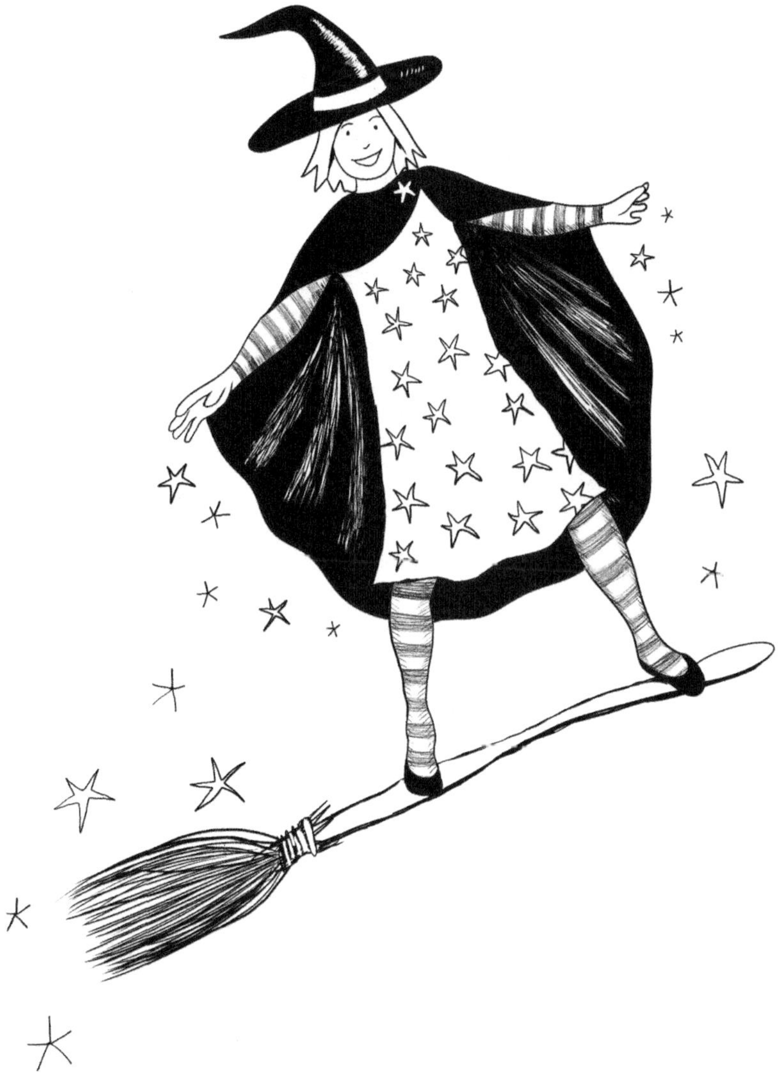

THE WITCH'S LOST CAT

Jack was finishing his homework at the dining room table when his Dad came home from work. As soon as his Dad walked in, he knew there was something wrong. Normally his Dad would give him a pat on his shoulder and ask him what sort of day he had had at school. Today his Dad had a sad face and went straight to his Mum, hugged her and whispered in her ear.

His Mum's hand shot to her mouth. 'Oh no!'

Jack looked at his parents.

'What's wrong?'

Jack's Dad took his Mum's hand and they sat at the table beside Jack.

'Dad, what's wrong?' Jack asked again.

His Dad looked at his Mum, then Jack, and said 'I got bad news at work today, if the company doesn't get any orders soon, we will be forced to close, and I'll be out of work. If that happens, we won't have much money to spend on holidays, birthdays or Christmas. However, let's wait and see what happens.'

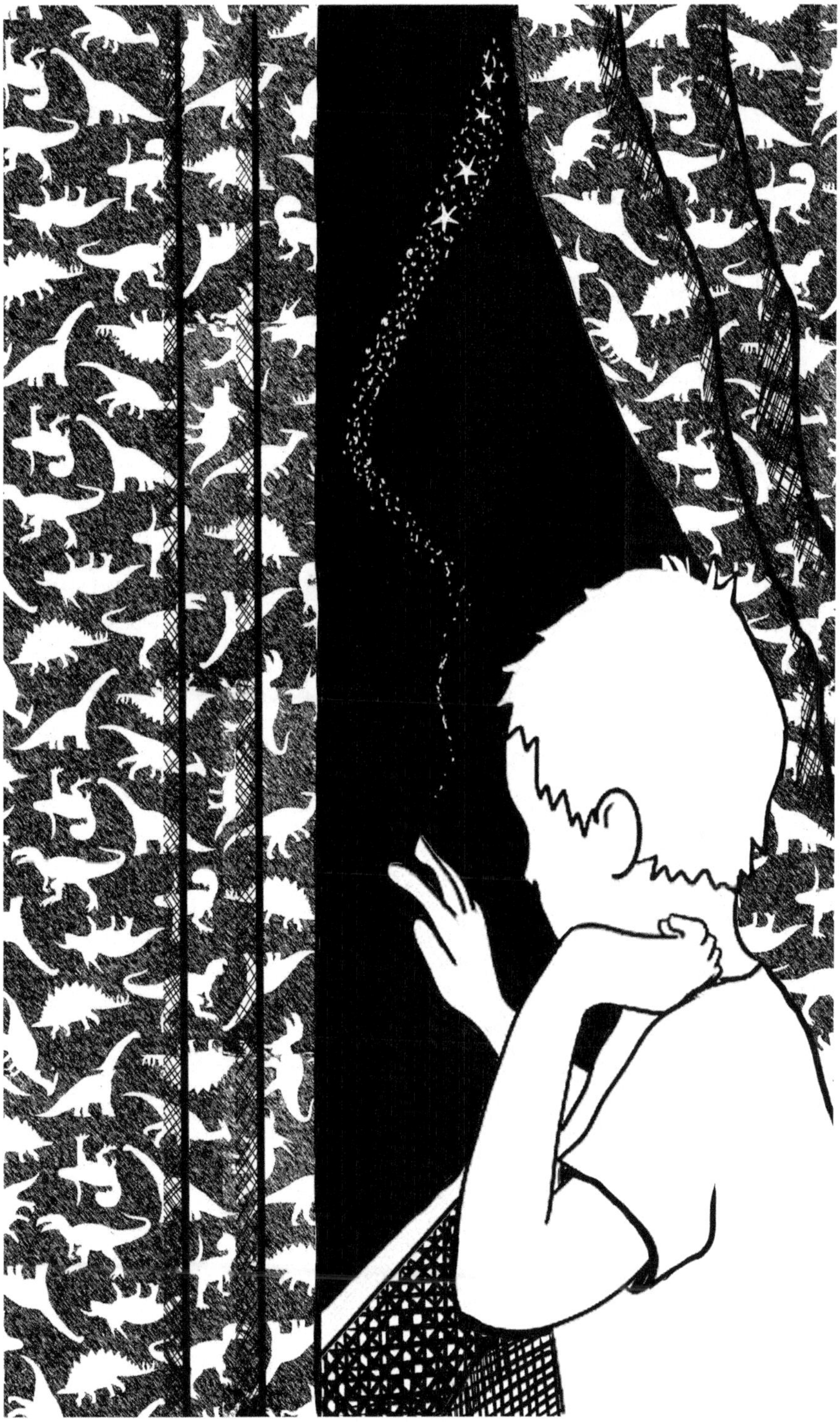

That night Jack went to bed but, try as he may, he could not stop thinking about his Dad.
Eventually Jack got out of bed and went over to the bedroom window.
The sky was jet black with lots of twinkling stars. Jack was staring out, deep in thought when he saw a bright light out of the corner of his eye. His first reaction was great, a shooting star, you don't see them often.

He turned his head to look at the shooting star, then thought. That's not a shooting star, it's a white trail zig zagging across the sky.

Jack was puzzled, he had never seen or heard of anything like this before. As he watched it got closer to Jack's house. Suddenly it zoomed towards Jack's bedroom window.

Jack was so surprised he took a step back into his room, then gasped.

Outside his window was a Witch sitting on a broomstick. She was looking straight at Jack and gesturing for him to open his window.

Jack shook his head, mainly to make sure he wasn't dreaming, then he pinched himself. No, he was wide awake.
The Witch gestured again so Jack went over and opened his window.
'I'm sorry to trouble you, but have you seen a black cat?' The Witch asked.
Jack shook his head and stuttered, 'N N No.'

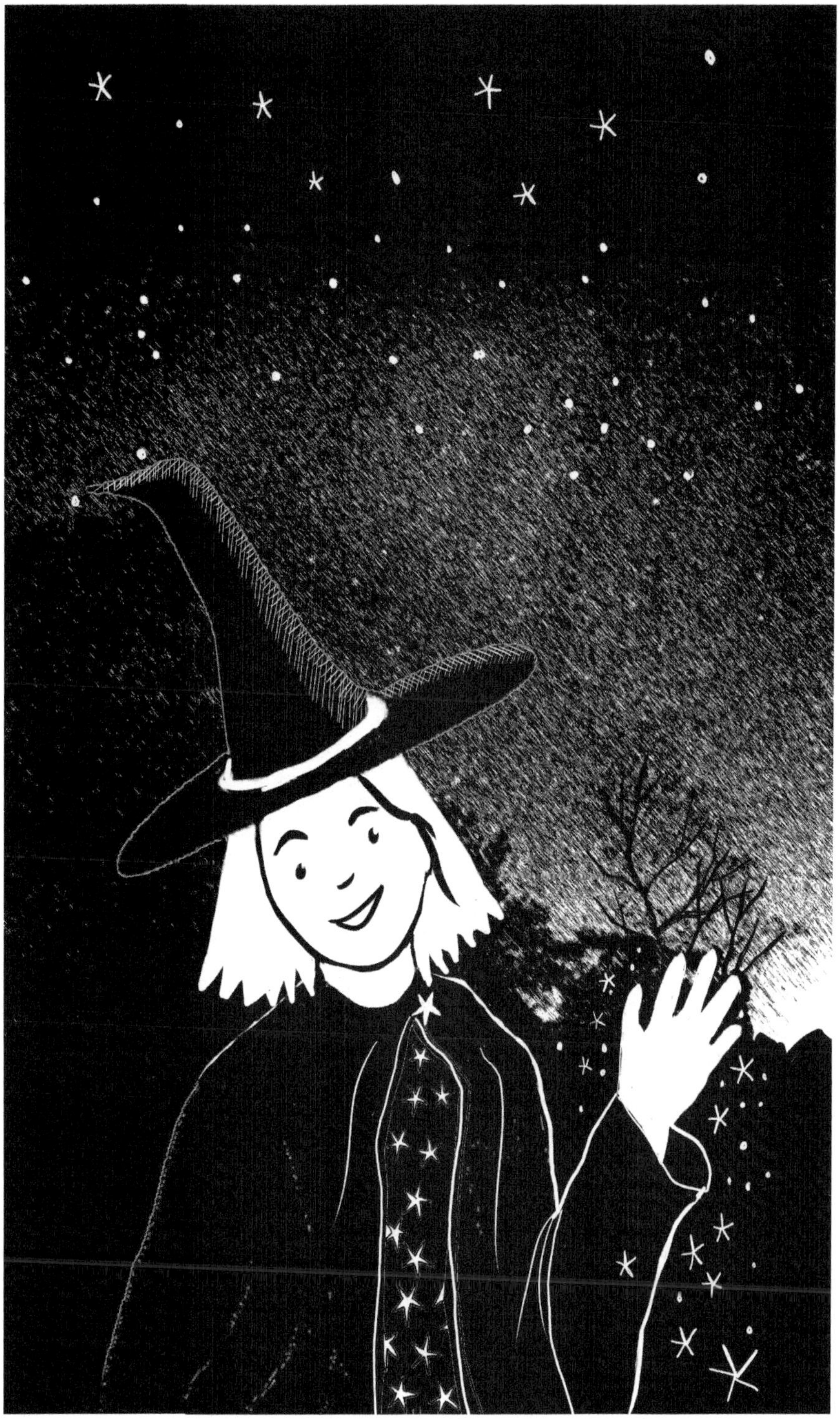

The Witch continued. 'We were flying over when this thing that looked like a giant spider flew right in front of us. I had to do an emergency stop on my broom. I flew on muttering about crazy flying spiders when I realised my cat Tom wasn't answering. I looked over my shoulder and he wasn't on the broom. He must have fallen off when I did my emergency stop. I've been back and called him but I can't find him. Can you help?'

Jack said. 'I'll try, I'll look tomorrow when I go to school, and I'll ask my friends to help too.'

The Witch smiled at Jack and said. 'You are a nice boy, thank you for offering to help. Remember the cat's name's Tom and he's like the sky, jet black. If you find him tell him he's to go with you and I'll come and pick him up. He understands humans and speaks, but only speaks to me.'

'Jack! It's getting late and I think you should be in bed' called his mother.

The Witch then said 'Sleep tight Jack, I'll see you tomorrow night.'

And with that the Witch turned and zoomed off, becoming a small dot of light until she was finally disappeared out of sight.

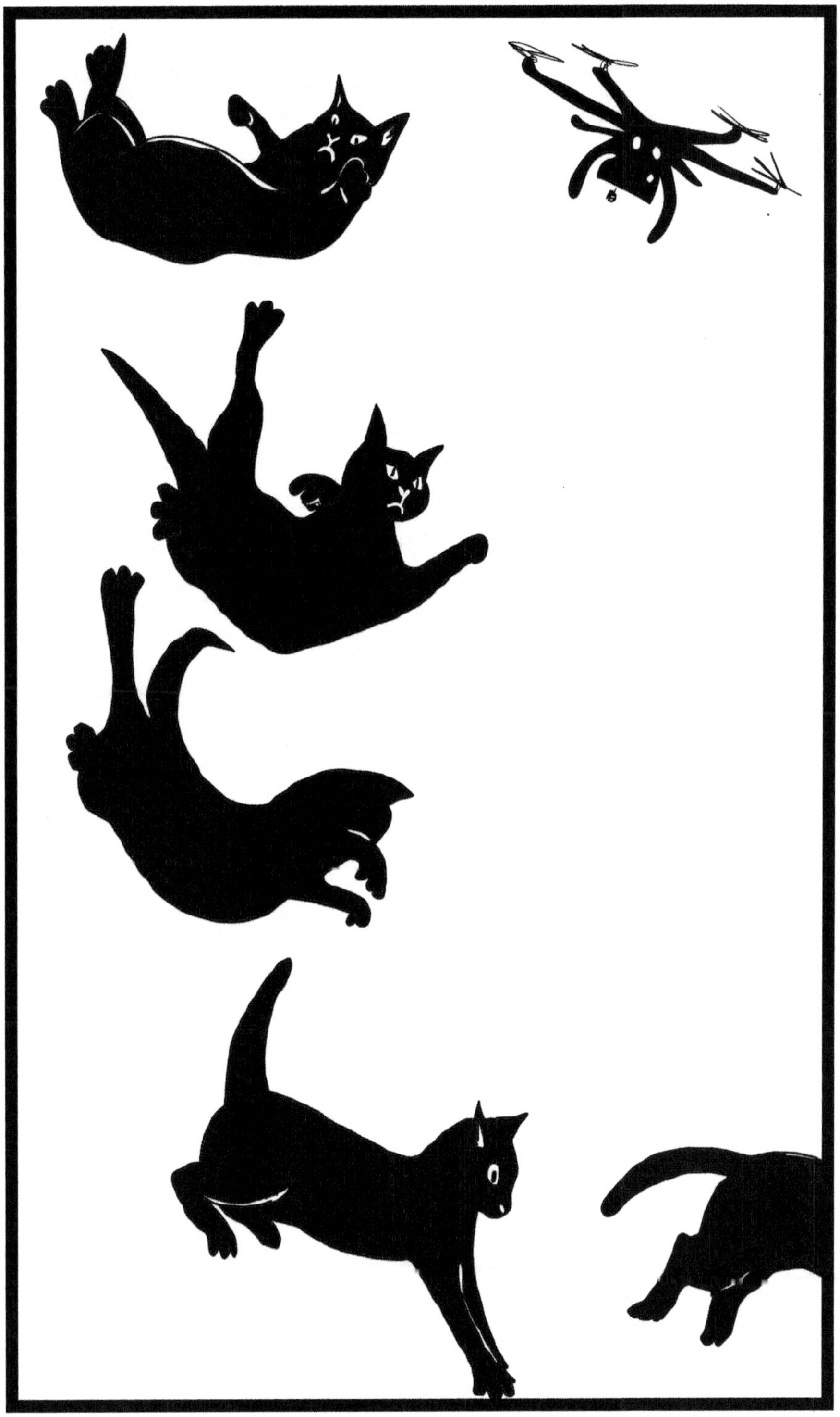

Next day at school Jack got his friends around him and told them about the Witch. Some just laughed and said. 'There are no such things as witches, or witches on broomsticks, it's only in fairy stories.'

'That's as may be but I'm still going to look for the cat,' said Jack.

However, most of Jack's friends agreed to help him look for Tom.

All day when they had time, they looked behind hedges, in bins, up trees, under cars any place a cat could crawl. But no luck.

That night when Jack went to bed, he waited at the bedroom window.

As he watched there was a sudden bright light and there was the Witch once again outside his window.

Jack opened the window to speak to the Witch.

'Hello Jack,' the Witch said. 'I can see by your face you haven't found Tom.'

'I'm sorry,' said Jack. 'My friends and I have looked everywhere, but we haven't found him.'

'Please don't worry, I'll keep searching, you get to bed, and I'll come back tomorrow night' the Witch replied.

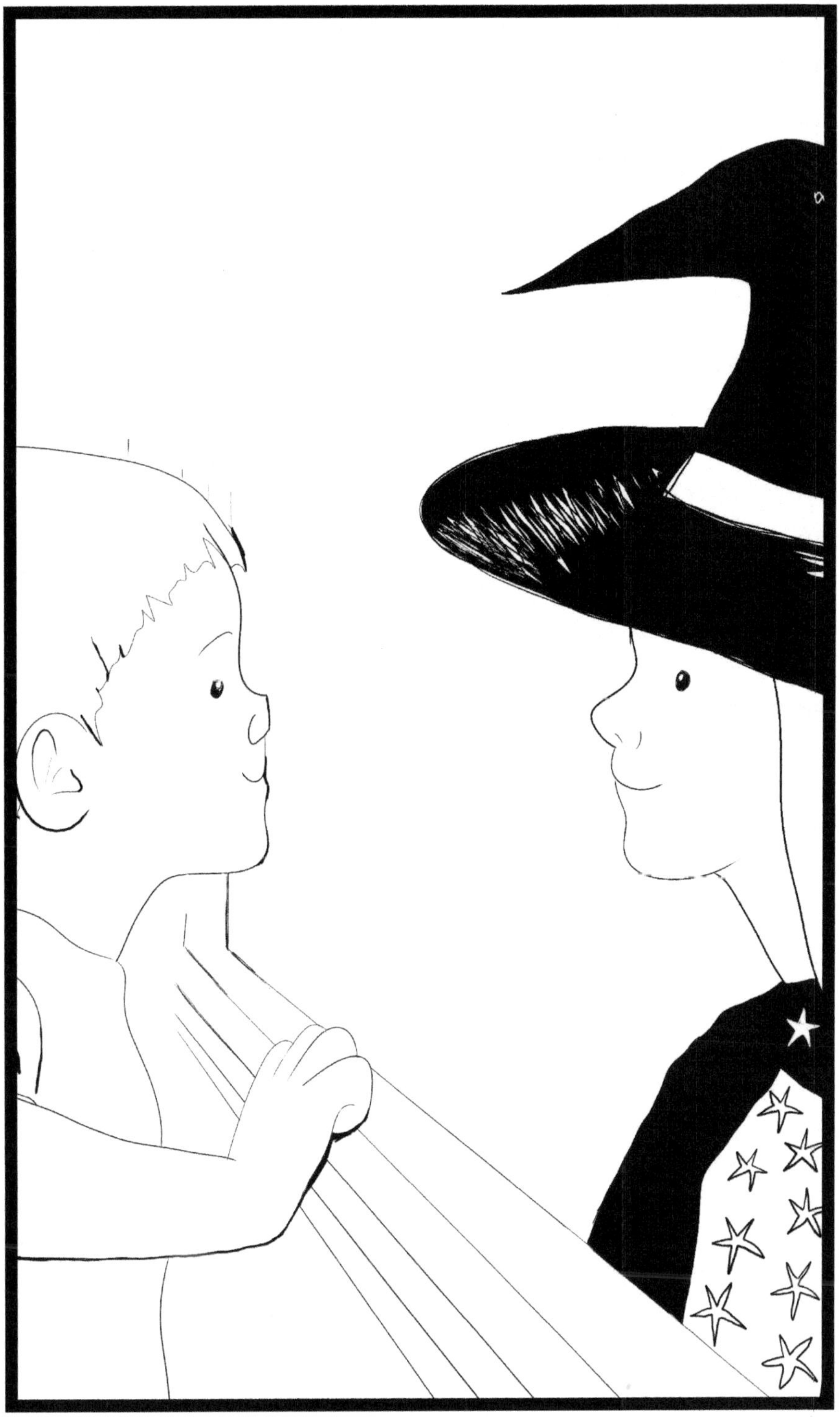

The next day Jack was heading home from school when he thought he heard a meow.

He stopped, listened and looked around, nothing.

He started to walk slowly when he heard it again, a quiet meow.

Jack looked around, trying to see where the meows were coming from.

They were coming from over there, inside a big refuse bin on wheels with a lid.

Jack went over and lifted the lid.

There, staring up at him, was an incredibly sad black cat covered in food waste which had matted his fur into spiked tufts.

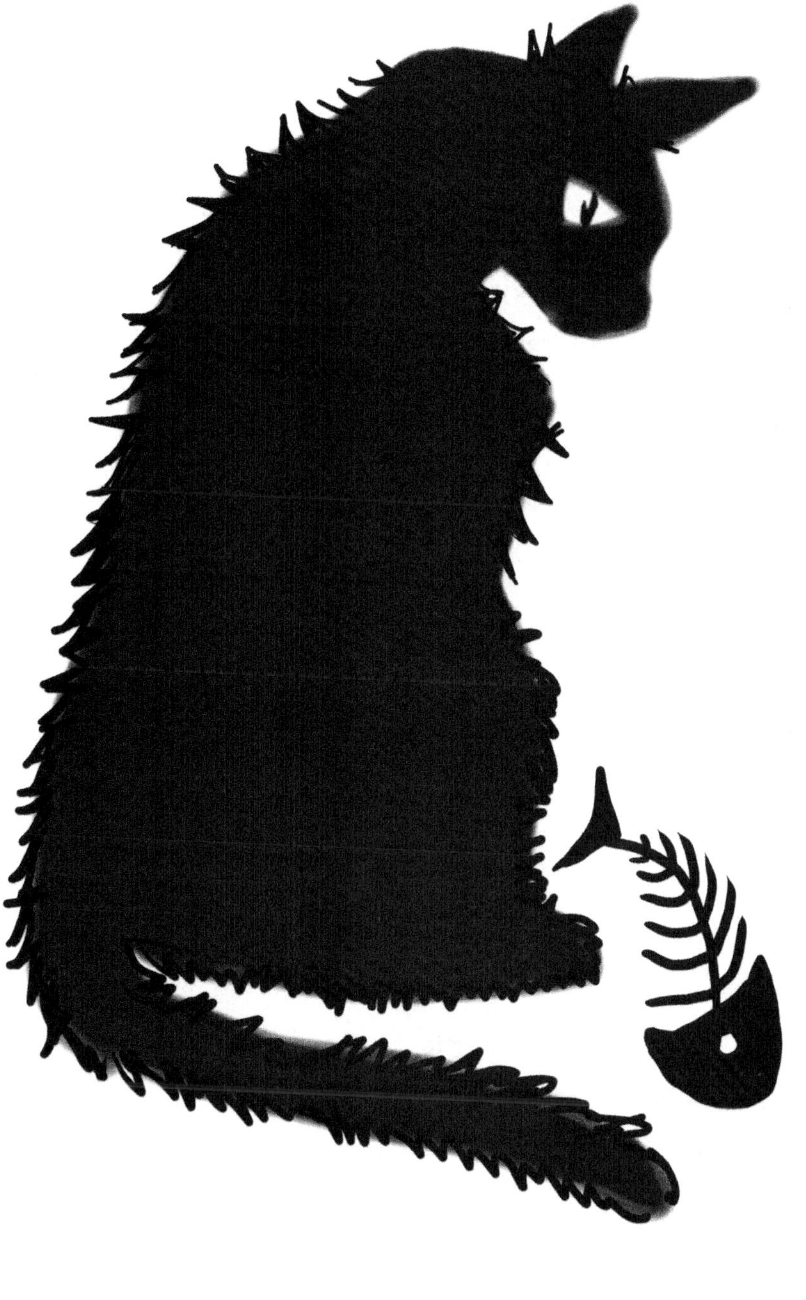

Jack reached in and lifted Tom out.

Tom's fur was matted with food, covered in sticky gravy, bits of carrots and he had a sprout leaf stuck to his nose, he smelt awful.

'Right,' Jack said. 'The Witch says you've to come with me and she'll pick you up tonight.'

Tom purred and rubbed himself against Jack.

'Before you do, no more rubbing. You smell. I need to get you back to my house and cleaned up.'

When Jack got home, he took Tom to the garden shed and locked him inside, so he would be safe, and no one would see him.

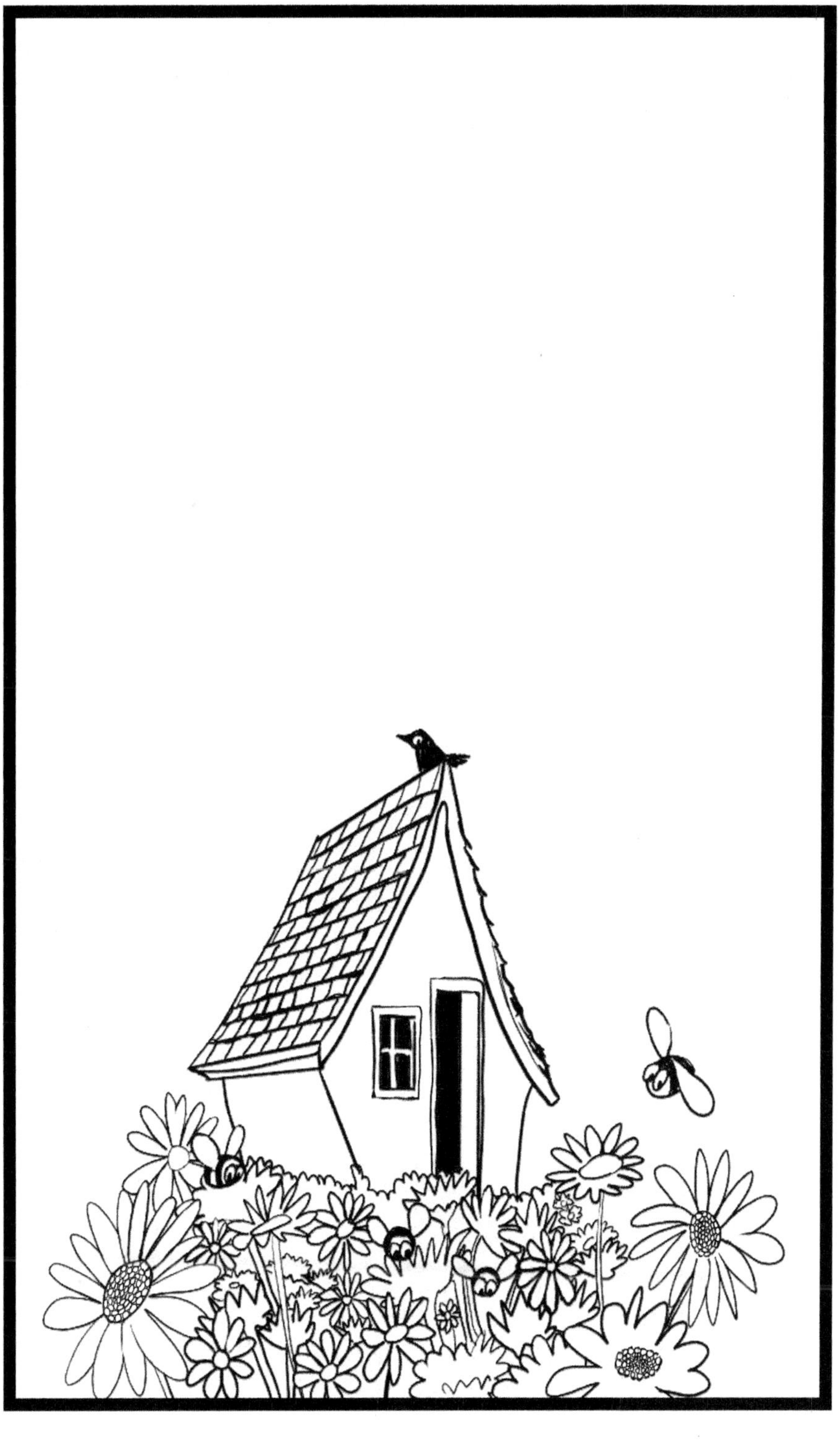

Later Jack crept out and took Tom into the house and upstairs to his bedroom.

That evening, while his parents were watching television, Jack went to his room, got Tom and took him to the bathroom, washed him then dried him with his mum's hairdryer.

When he was finished, he looked at Tom.

'No wonder the Witch misses you, you are such a beautiful cat. Your fur is glowing now you're clean. Let's go to the window to watch for the Witch.'

They both went to the bedroom window, Tom flicking his tail while standing on the window sill when suddenly, in a flash of light, the Witch was there sitting on her broomstick smiling at Jack and Tom.

'You found him' she exclaimed. 'Tom I've been ever so worried. Are you hurt?'

Tom moved to the open window and purred and meowed at the Witch.

'I know you fell off. It was that stupid flying spider's fault,' she replied.

Jack cleared his throat then spoke. 'I think your flying spider was a drone which I suppose could look like a giant spider.'

'Either way' the Witch replied. 'It was in my air space, forced me to brake, and caused Tom to fall off. Any way it's worked out alright, Tom's had an adventure and I have a new friend. I would like to thank you for rescuing Tom. I can grant you a wish. Go on, go ahead, wish and I'll see what I can do.'

The Witch was silent and gave Jack a long stare. 'Are you sure that's what you want to wish?'

'Yes' answered Jack.

'Okay Jack I'll try my best' said the Witch. 'Anyway, Tom and I need to go. Bye Jack and thanks again for your help.'

Tom turned, rubbed his face against Jack's, then spun around and lightly jumped onto the back of the broomstick. Tom raised a paw to wave, then in the blink of an eye, they were gone.

Jack watched a white light flash across the sky (which was the Witch and Tom) until it disappeared, then went to bed and fell asleep.

The next day Jack was finishing his homework when his Dad came home early from work. His Dad grabbed Jack's Mum and spun her around.

'We got a big order. All our jobs are safe! Lets go out for dinner to celebrate. Jack where would you like to go?' Jack said just two words. 'Pizza please!'

Later that night when Jack was in bed, he thought about the Witch and Tom, and silently thanked them for granting his wish.

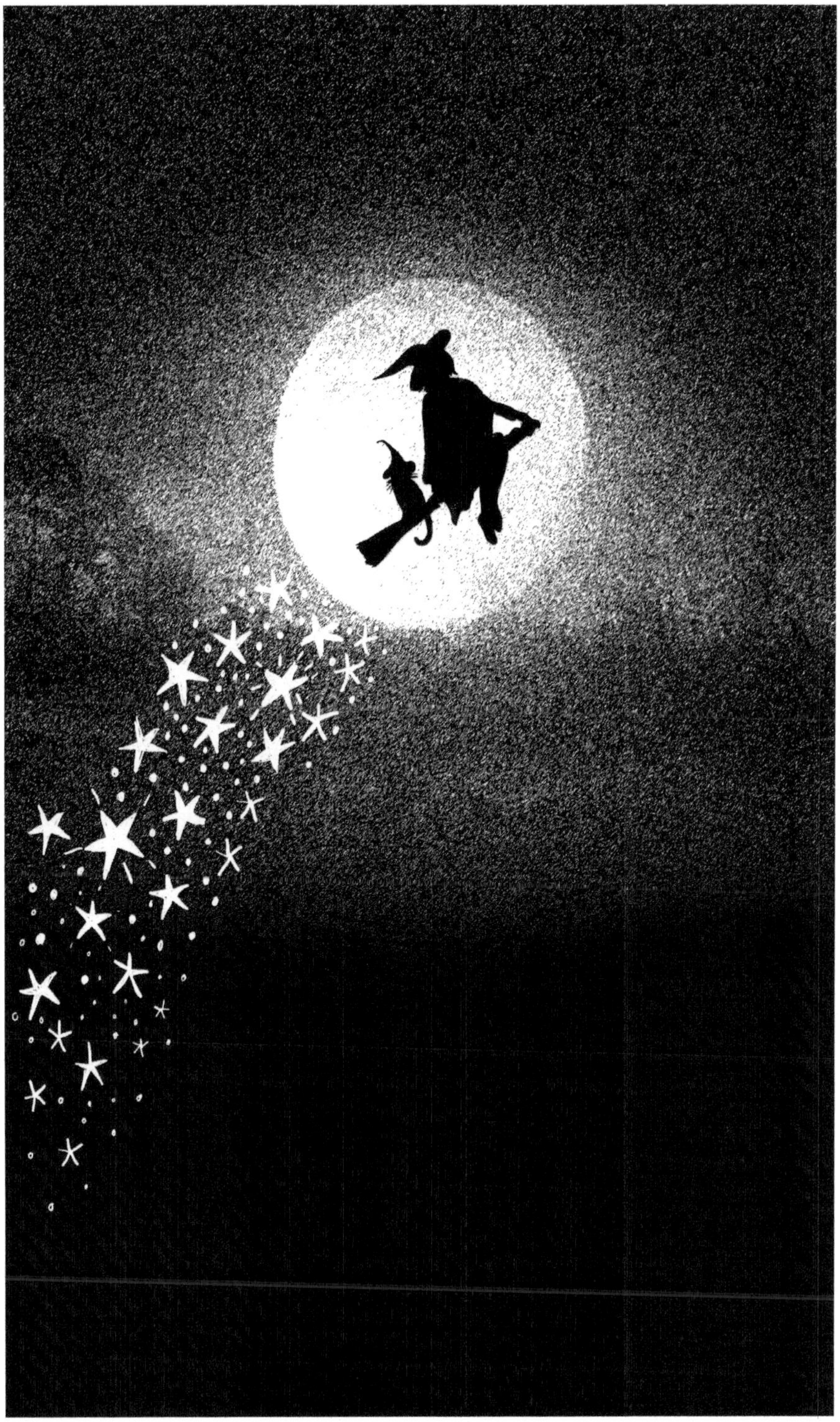

THE WITCH'S BROKEN BROOM

Jack was finishing his breakfast before he went to school. He was deep in thought. Had he finished all his homework, packed his gym kit and most importantly, put his packed lunch in his backpack? He mentally ticked off all these things.

Out of the corner of his eye he saw a movement outside on the windowsill.

He turned his head to look.

There sitting on the sill waving a paw at him was Tom the Witch's cat.

Jack looked around the kitchen. The only other person in the house was his mother, and she was upstairs getting ready to go to work.

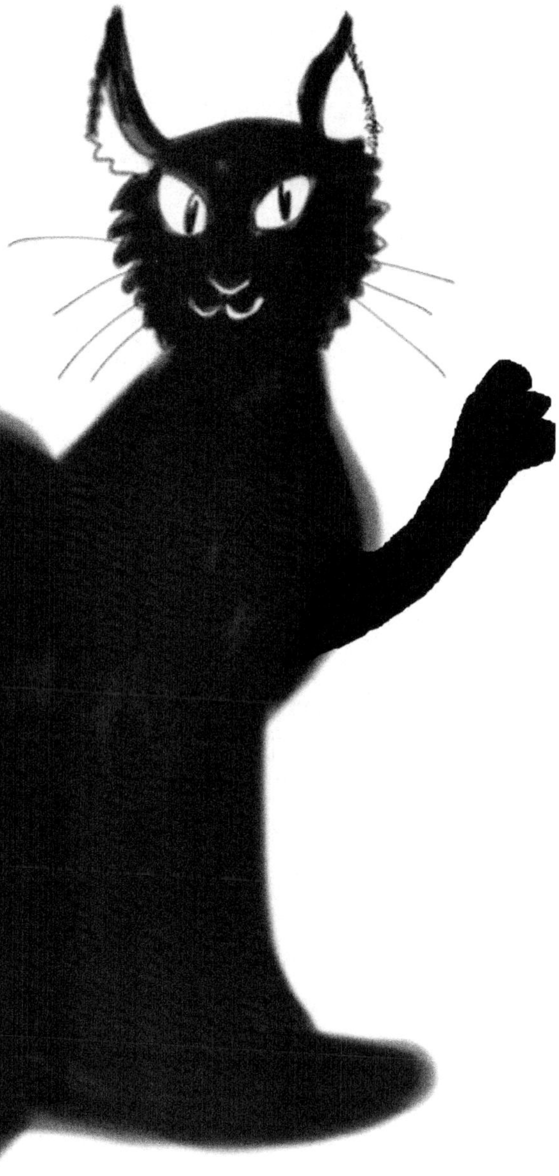

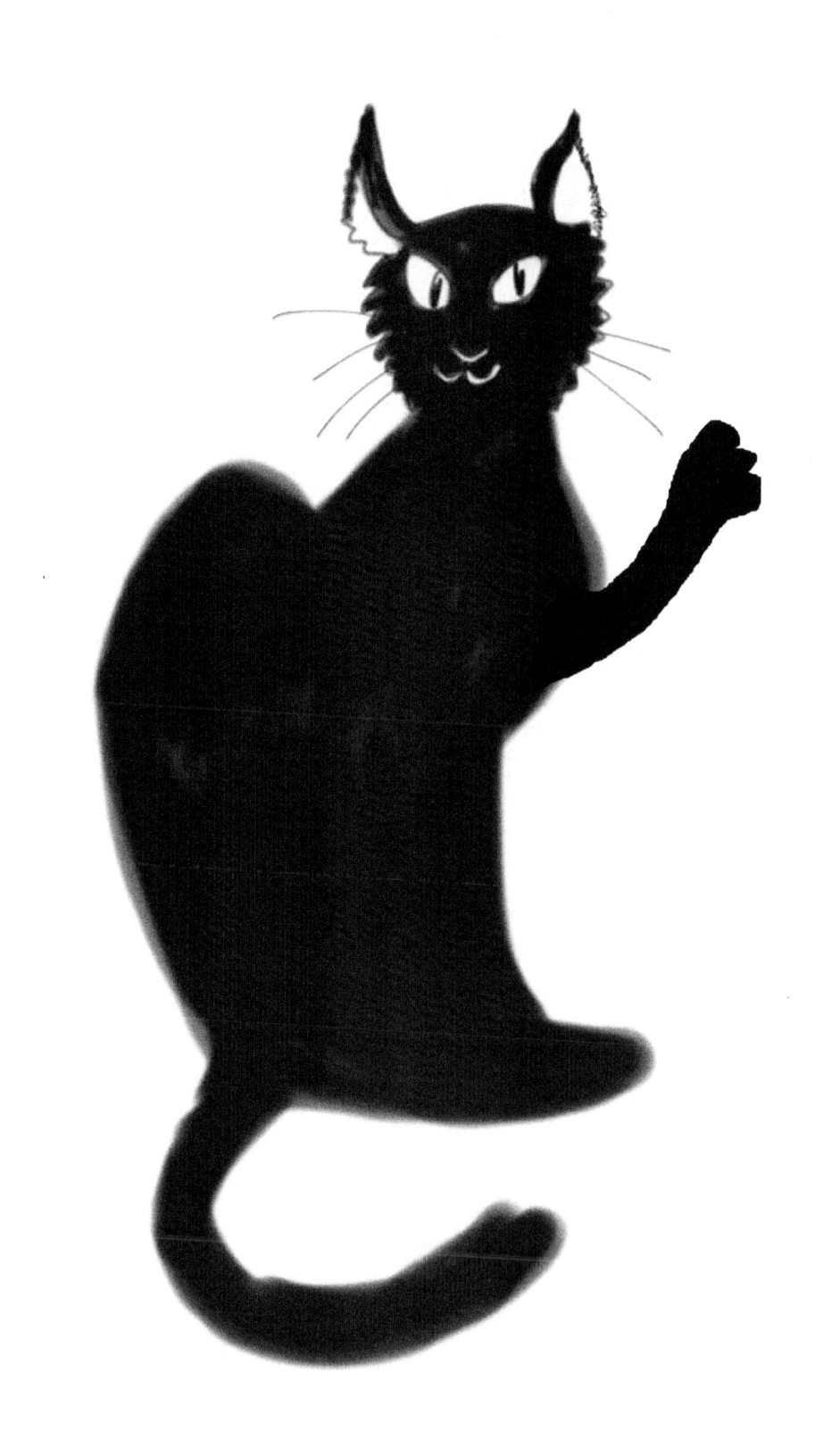

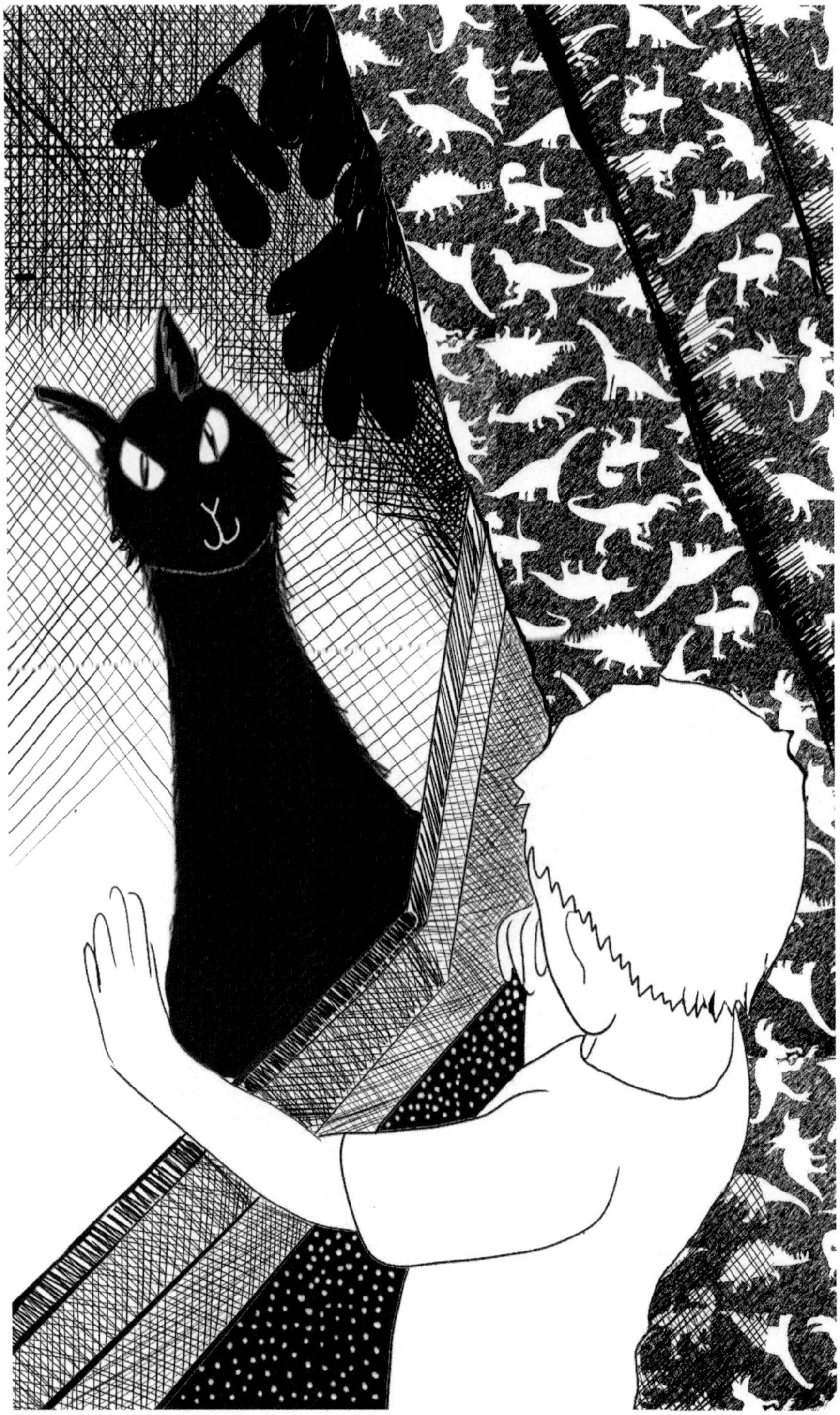

Jack quickly put on his jacket, grabbed his school bag, shouted 'Goodbye' to his mum then shot out of the door.

Tom was waiting for him.

Jack reached down, lifted Tom and gave him a cuddle.

'Tom, it's great to see you but what are you doing here without the Witch?' asked Jack.

Tom jumped out of Jack's arms then ran to the corner of the house, while Jack followed on.

When Jack got to the corner, he watched Tom head to some bushes, where, crouched down peering out, was the Witch.

When the Witch saw Jack, she stood up ran towards him then grabbed his hand.

'Jack, I'm glad Tom got you, I need your help again.'

'You, you need my help!' Jack stuttered. 'You're a Witch, you can do magic and cast all sorts of spells, why do you need my help?

The Witch smiled and said 'Witches can do all those things, but there are things we use like brooms and clothes, we can only get those from special witches.'

She sighed.

'Tom and I were flying last night when one of these drone things flew in front of us, I had to swerve to miss it and flew into a building. When we hit the building, my broom snapped into three pieces and Tom and I fell and hit the ground.'

Tom purred.

'Tom was lucky, being a cat, he twisted in mid-air then landed on his four paws. I flailed and flapped as I fell, then landed on my bottom.'

Tom purred again. Jack thought it sounded like Tom was laughing.

'Apart from having a sore bottom, I'm okay, but the broom is ruined. Can you help me get to the witch that makes the brooms?'

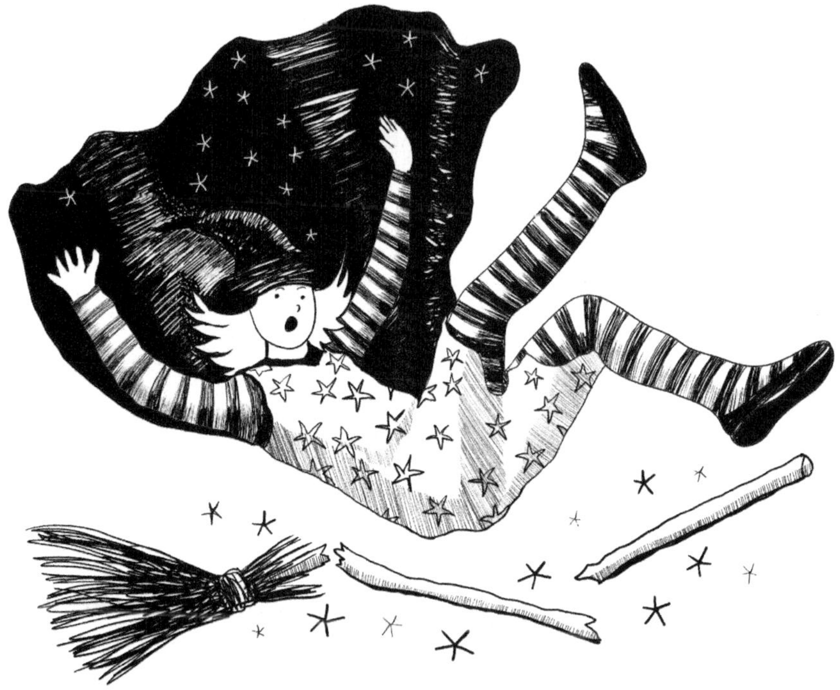

Jack smiled. 'Of course I will, but I need to go to school today. Will it be okay if we do it tomorrow as it's Saturday?'

'Thanks Jack. We'll need some place to hide until tomorrow then?' she asked.

'Follow me' Jack said as he led them to the back of the house, 'You can stay in the garden shed until tomorrow, then we can go to get a new broom.'

The Witch and Tom went into the shed, saw a canvas seat and sat down.

As Jack turned to go, he stopped. He fished inside his school bag and brought out his packed lunch. He offered it to the Witch.

'I can't take your lunch Jack,' the Witch said.

'Please take it, I've got my pocket money and can buy my lunch at school,' Jack insisted.

'Thank you. You are very kind, Tom and I both appreciate your help, don't we Tom?'

Tom gave a meow and rubbed himself along Jack's legs.

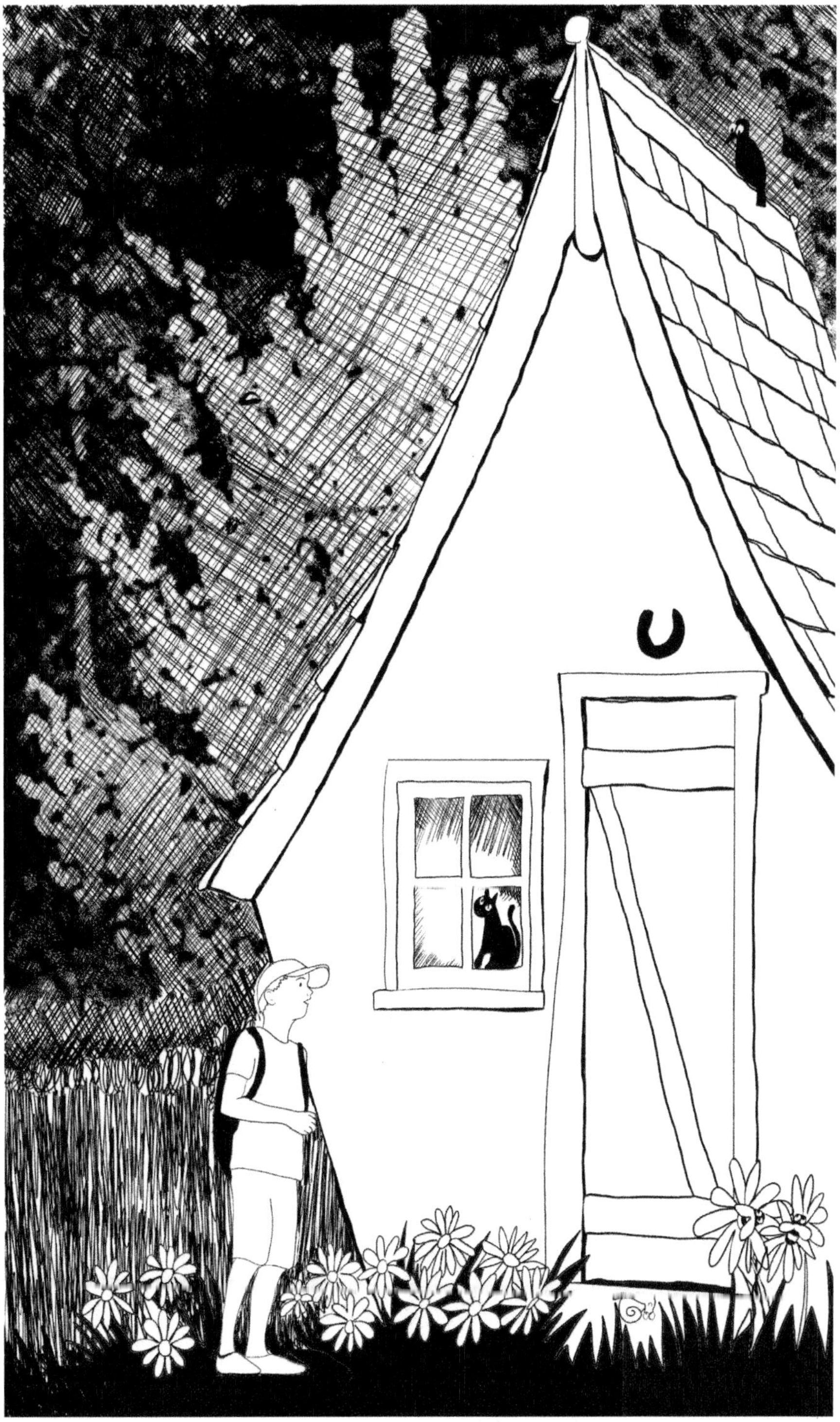

The next day Jack got up early put some of his old clothes into his backpack and told his parents he was going for a walk with his friends.

He crept out to the shed so his parents wouldn't see him.

In the shed he opened his backpack taking out his old clothes and some food he brought from the house.

He asked the Witch to wear his old clothes as it would look funny to see a Witch walking through the town.

The Witch hesitated, looked at Tom then said, 'I can't change my clothes Jack. These are magic clothes. I can't do magic without them.'

'But you can't walk through the town dressed like that' Jack replied. 'You'll draw attention to us. People don't see witches walking around. As soon as we find the broom, Witch, you can change back to your witch's clothes.'

Tom meowed to the Witch.

'OK' the Witch said. 'Tom agrees with you, it's the best thing to do, to get across town. If you wait outside, I'll get changed.'

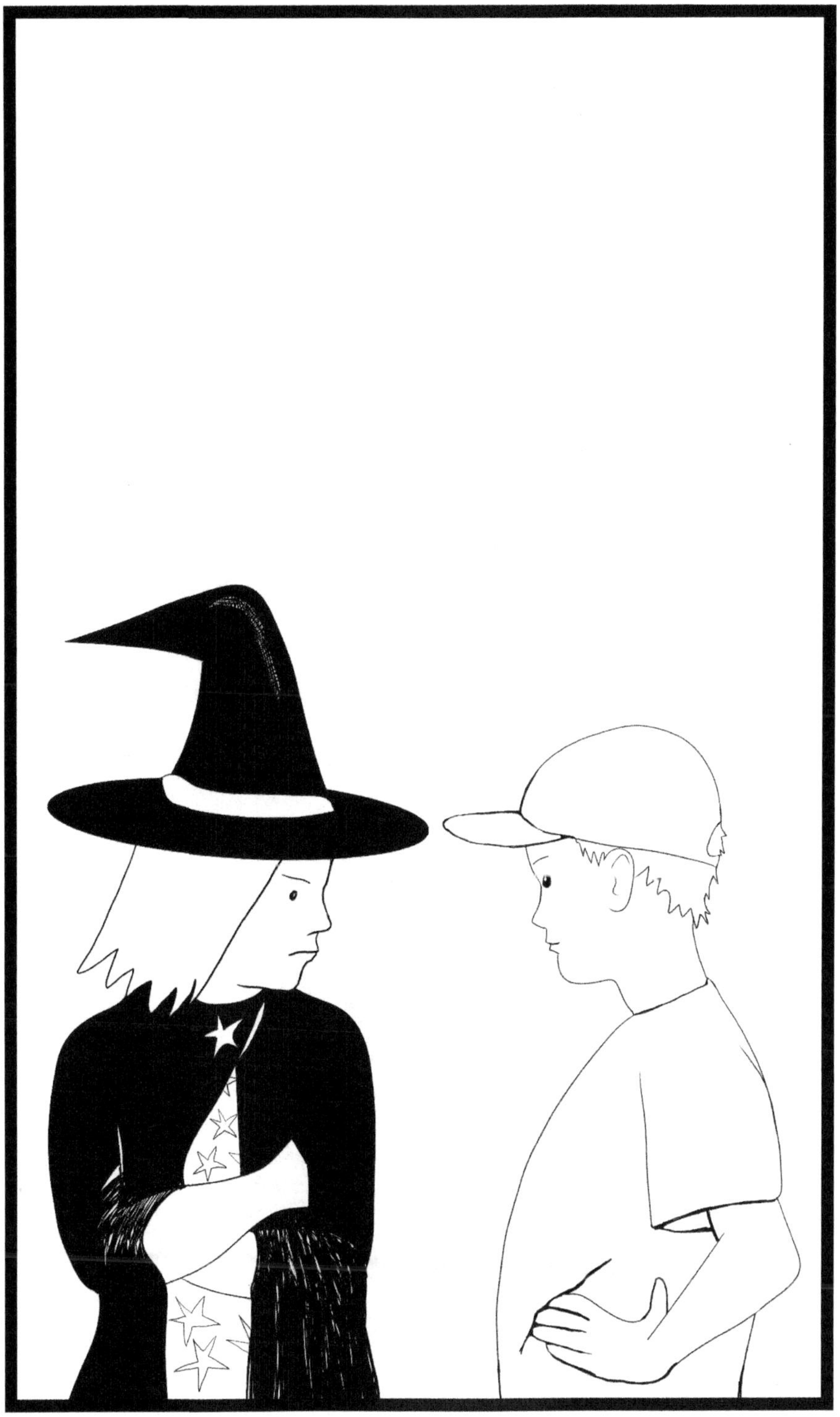

When the Witch had changed, she opened the shed door and stepped out, Jack stood back in amazement.

The Witch was about the same size as him and it was funny to see her in his clothes.

'Don't you dare laugh at me,' she said.

'Here, let me put my clothes in your backpack, I don't know what would happen if you touched them. The magic might work with you. Anyway, lets go.'

Jack put Tom into his backpack on top of the Witch's clothes but left the top open so Tom could look out.

They were halfway across town heading to the woods when Jack saw Tommy Smith and his gang of bullies.

Jack stopped, looking around for a way to avoid them.

The Witch stopped with Jack.

Looking at him she asked. 'What is it? You look frightened.'

'Tommy Smith and his gang,' Jack hissed.

The Witch watched as the gang moved towards them swaggering as they met. By their manner it was obvious they were going to cause trouble.

The Witch quietly said to Jack. 'Reach into your backpack and hold my clothes and hold my hand.'

Jack quickly reached into the backpack and squeezed a handful of the material while holding the Witch's hand.

The gang were moving into position to surround Jack and the Witch when they disappeared. They looked around in amazement looking for them, but they were nowhere to be seen.

Meantime the Witch whispered in Jack's ear.

'Let's have some fun, here's what we'll do.'

Jack had to stop himself laughing out when he heard what the Witch said.

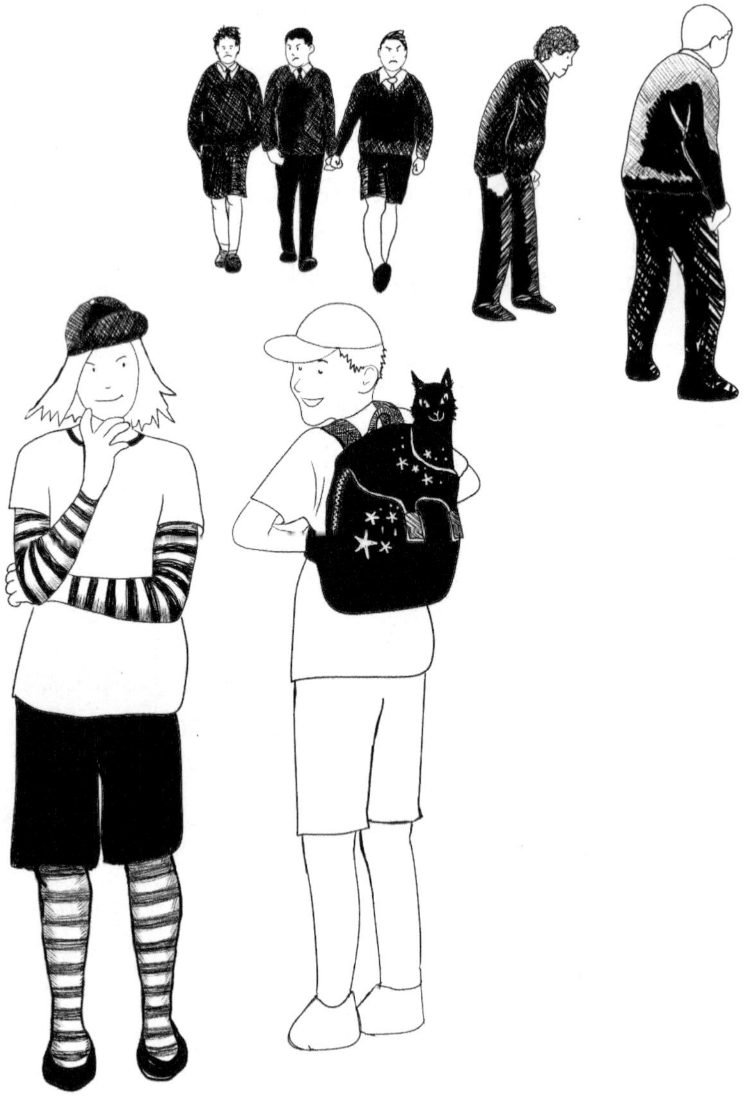

Tommy was looking round trying to see where Jack had gone when he leapt forward and turned on his gang.

'Right who kicked me on the bottom, that was sore and I'm going to punch who did it!' He snarled.

The gang all looked at each other, no one had kicked Tommy, they knew better.

They were looking around when Ben Straw, another member of the gang, shouted out.

'Someone just twisted my ear, that was sore. Who did it?'

Suddenly another member of the gang shouted 'Ouch, someone stamped on my foot. I'm not hanging around, something strange is going on, I'm off!'

With that he ran off, followed by the rest of the gang.

Tommy Smith was left on his own, looking around, wondering, what was going to happen next when suddenly Jack and The Witch appeared in front of him.

Tommy backed away as Jack and The Witch walked towards him.

'What's wrong Tommy?' asked Jack. 'Something strange happen to you and your gang?' he laughed.

'Well it did, my friend here has given me magic power to deal with bullies. If you or your gang bully me or any kids at school, the next time I'll use my magic powers to pull your trousers down in the playground. Now push off and don't annoy me or my friends again.'

'Yes, yes okay!' Tommy shouted as he ran away.

Jack, the Witch and Tom burst out laughing at Tommy as he tripped on the pavement, staggered, then ran around the corner.

'That was awesome.' Jack said. 'I could only dream of being able to do that to Tommy and his gang.'

'Before we go on,' the Witch said,' I want to give you the power to speak to Tom. He thought it was awesome too, didn't you Tom?'

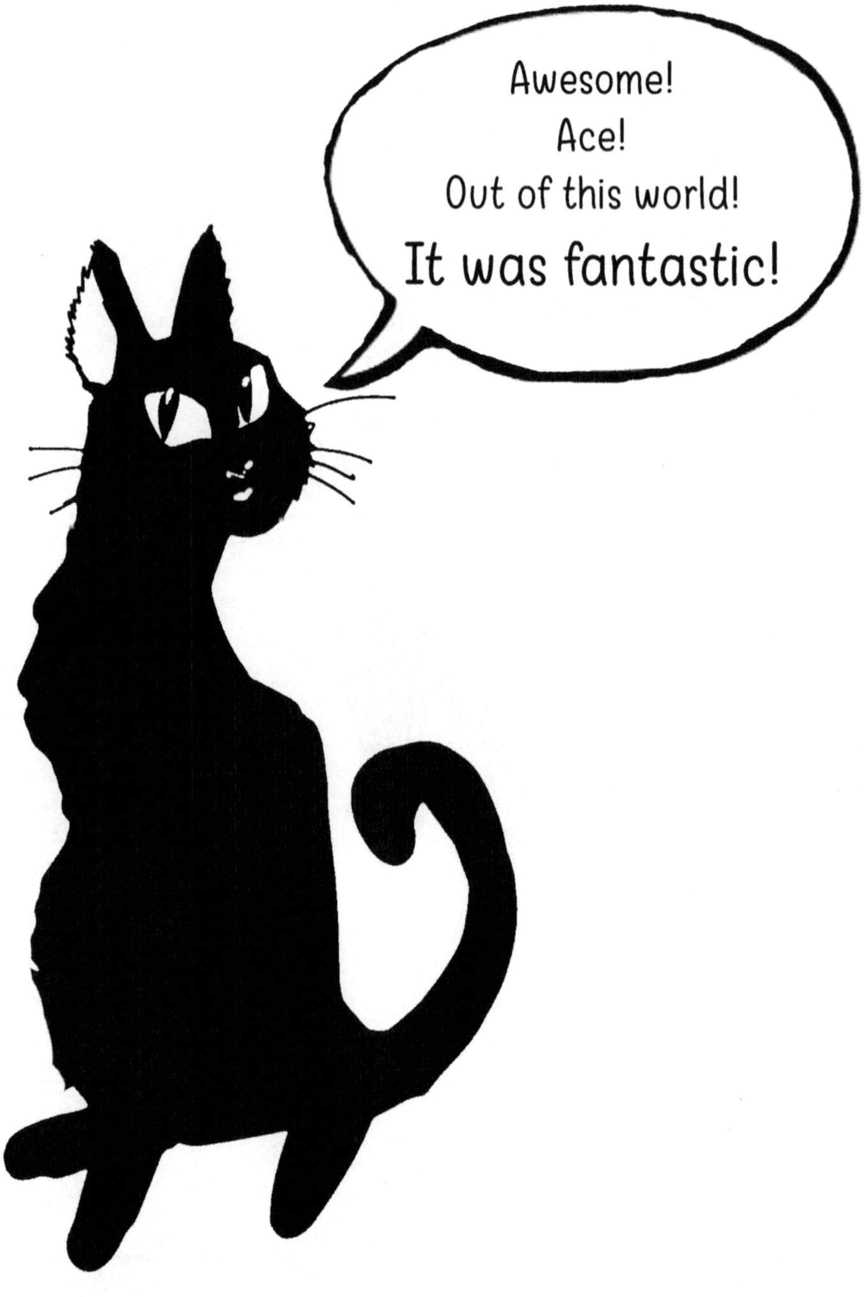
Awesome!
Ace!
Out of this world!
It was fantastic!

Tom leaned out off the backpack looked Jack in the face and replied, 'Awesome, ace, out of this world. It was fantastic.'

Jack swung the backpack off his shoulder and held it in front looking at Tom.

'Tom did you say all that?'

'Of course, I did, the Witch has given you the power so we can speak,' Tom replied.

'Come on let's go and get a new broom so I can get flying once more with the Witch.'

Jack shook his head; this was becoming a weird day he thought. He swung the backpack with Tom inside onto his shoulder then followed the Witch.

Jack and Tom talked all the way to the woods, Tom asking Jack about his family, friends and school, while Jack was interested in what it was like being a Witch's cat.

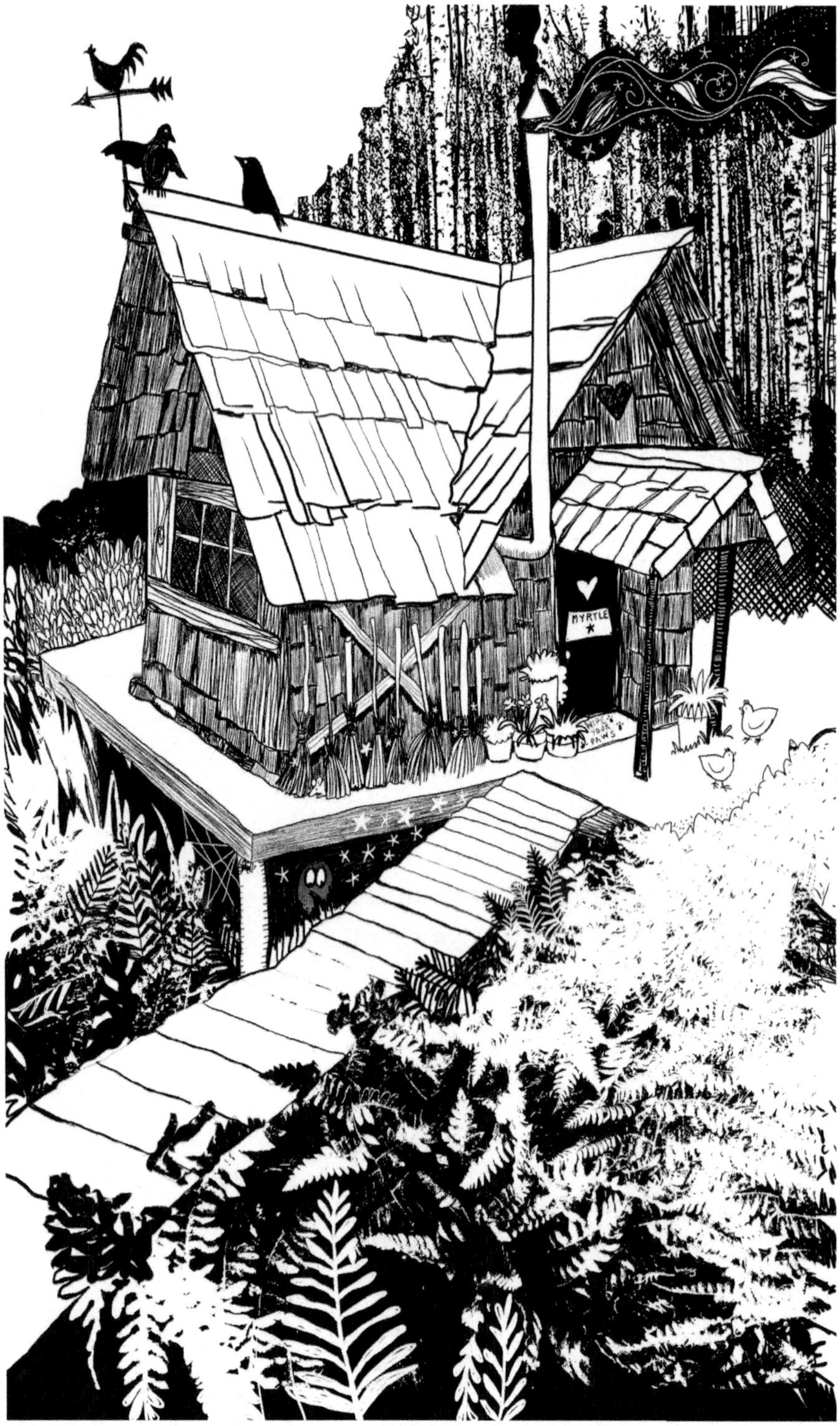
MYRTLE
WIPE YOUR PAWS

When they got to the woods the Witch walked them down secret trails until they came to a small clearing. In the centre of the clearing was a small hut with a collection of brooms of various sizes leaning on the wall.

The Witch rubbed her hands and ran across the clearing to the hut shouting 'Myrtle, it's me! I've come for a new broom.'

A wizened old woman with a stoop came out of the door and peered at the Witch. When she saw who it was her crinkled face lit up and she smiled.

'What happened to your broom and where are your Witch clothes?' she asked. 'Do you think all I have to do is make new brooms for you young Witches? I have a busy life and lots of spells to make.'

'Myrtle' the Witch replied. 'You know you love it when we need to come back for new brooms or spells.'

Myrtle laughed.

'Anyway, I've brought a friend with me so don't be rude or grumpy. This is Jack, who is a good friend and helped me get here. While I change into my Witch clothes in your shed, have a word with Jack.'

Myrtle looked at Jack and waved him over with a bony hand. Jack walked over with trepidation. This witch seemed a bit scary.

'Take my hand young man.'

Jack took her hand and as he did, he felt something strange happening to his body, he felt as if the old Witch could read his mind.

The old Witch smiled and let go of Jack's hand.

'You're right' she said to the Witch as she came out of the hut in her witch's clothes. 'He is a good friend and a nice person. Now let's sort you out with a broom.'
Jack looked on as the Witch and Tom selected various brooms and flew them in swoops and turns around the clearing.

When they picked a broom they liked, they thanked the old witch who gave Jack a wave then went into her shed to make spells.

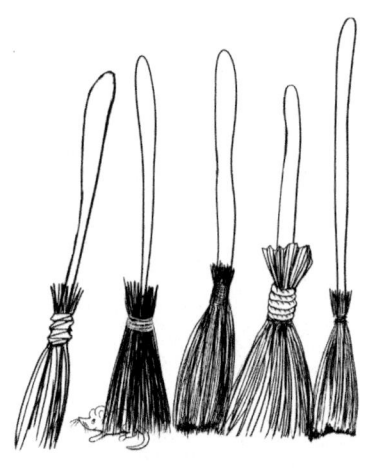

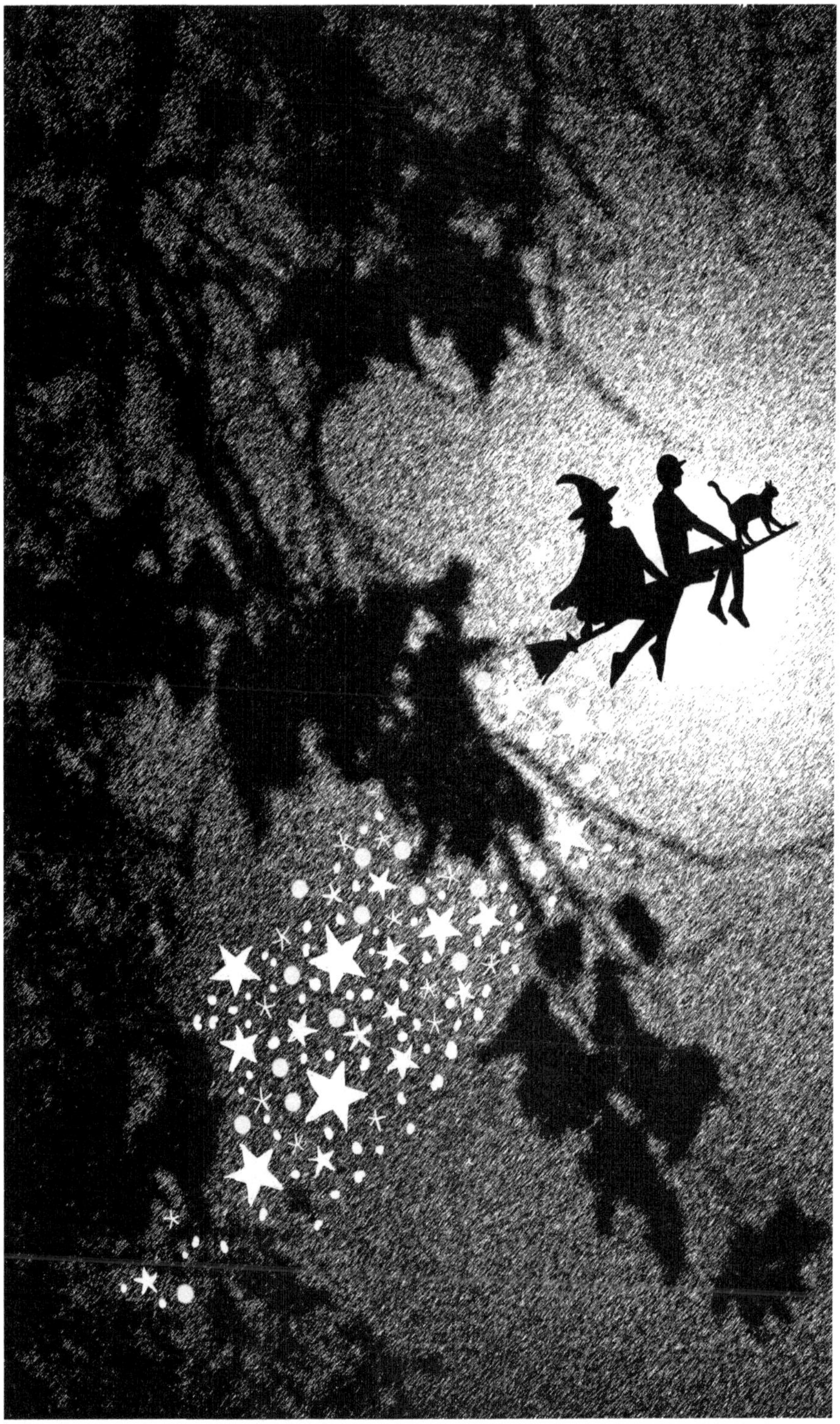

'Jack' the Witch said. 'Tom and I would like to thank you for helping us, what wish would you like?'

Jack smiled and replied, 'Nothing thank you, I've had great fun being with you and Tom, although it would be pretty cool if you could give me a lift home on your new broom.'

The Witch and Tom just smiled and said in unison 'Jump on let's go!'
With that the trio sat on the broom. The Witch looked over her shoulder to make sure everyone was safely on, then with a blink of an eye they were gone.

Minutes later they landed behind Jack's garden shed. Reluctantly Jack hopped of the broom disappointed that his flight was over so soon.

The Witch knew what Jack was thinking.

'Don't worry Jack, there'll be other trips and adventures in the future when you can ride the broom. Come on give Tom and me a high five before we take off.'

They gave each other a high five, then with a whoosh the Witch and Tom were gone.

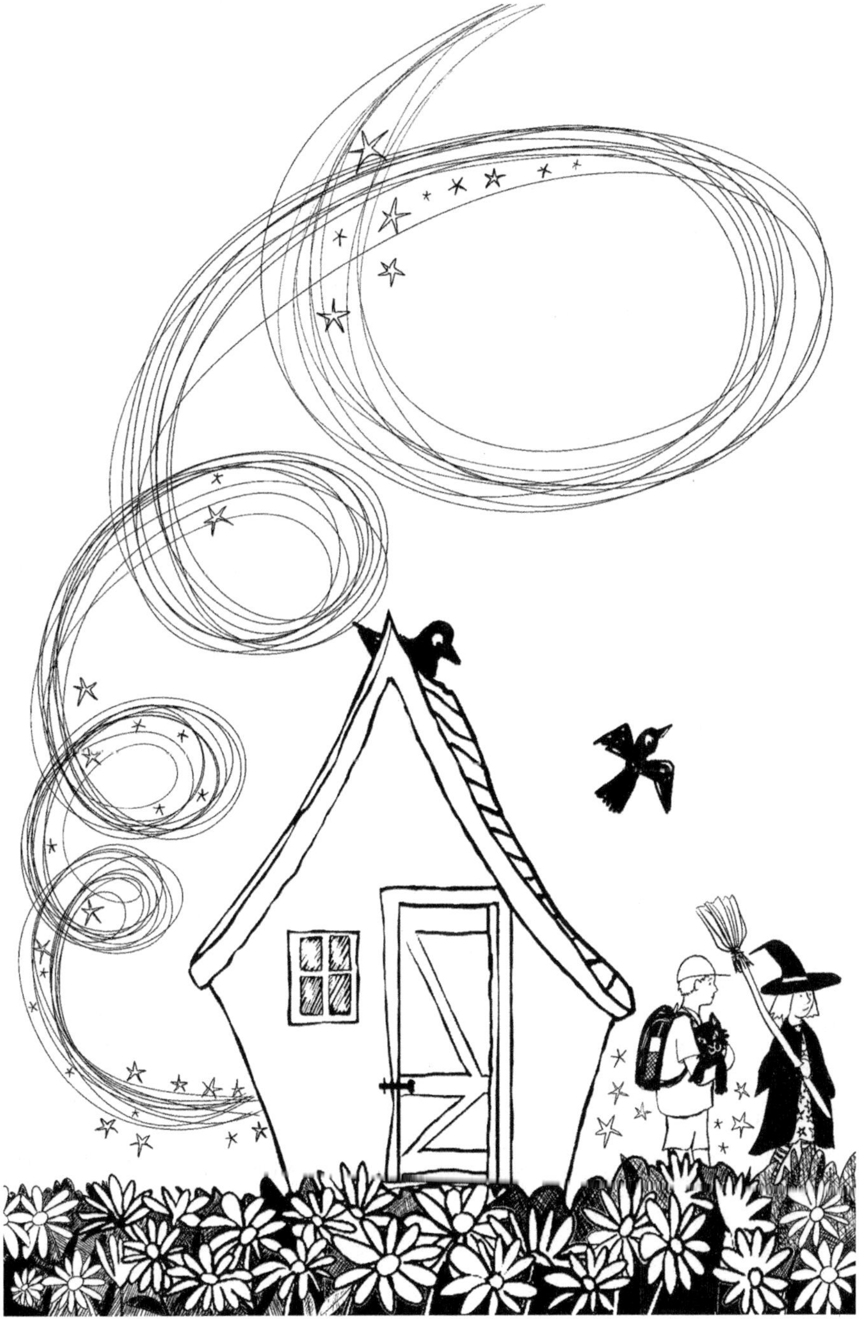

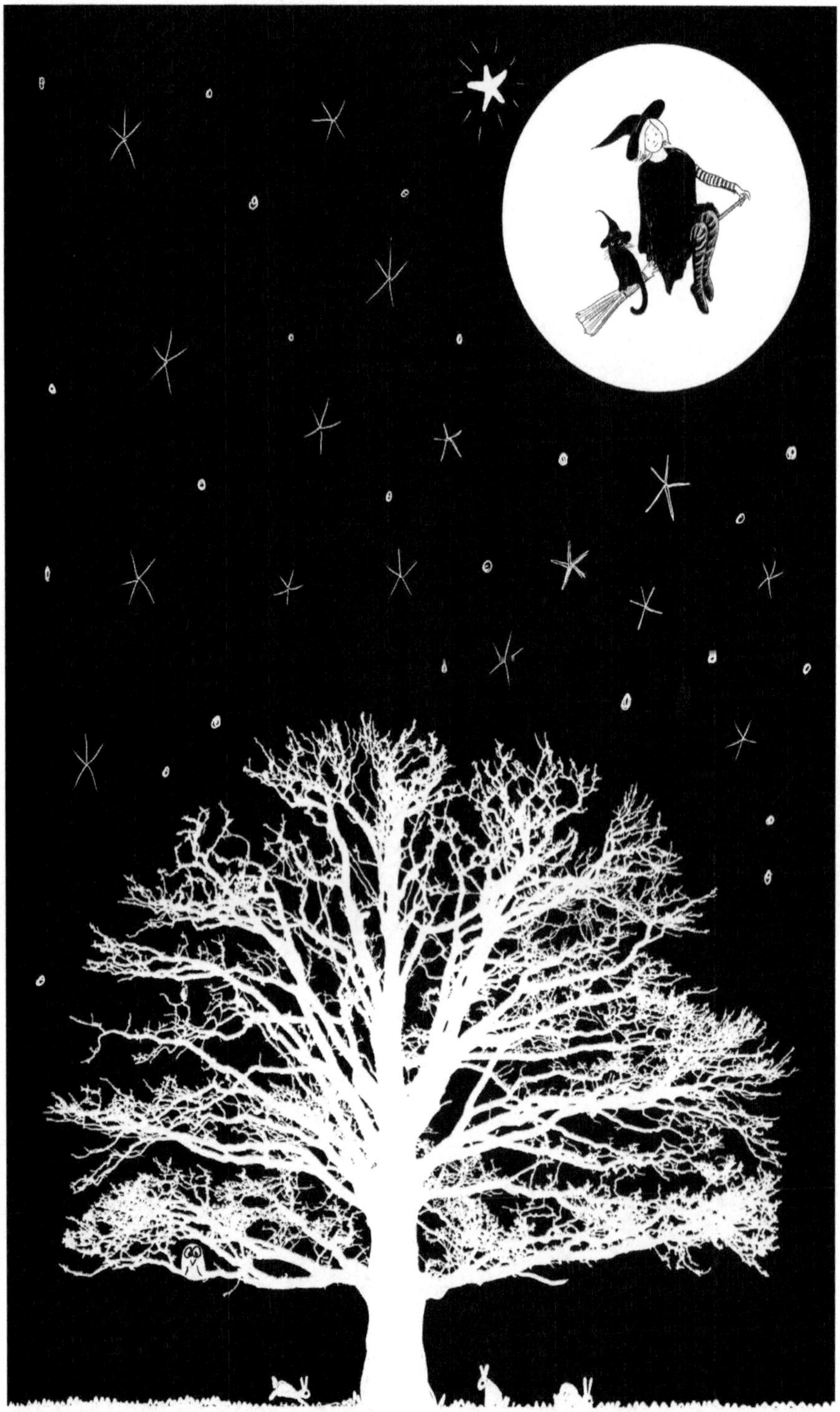

THE MISSING STAR

The Witch and Tom were flying through the night sky amongst the stars testing the new broom. They had crashed the previous broom and their friend Jack had helped them reach the magic wood where Myrtle the Broom Witch had given them this new one.

They were zipping amongst the stars twisting and turning putting the broom through its paces.

They were enjoying themselves whooping and laughing as the broom twisted and turned.

As they passed a star the Witch looked over her shoulder to ask Tom what he thought of the broom.

As she did Tom's eyes opened wide and he shouted.

'Look out! The star!'

The Witch quickly turned her head to see that they were heading straight for the star. She pulled the broom into a sharp turn, but, too late. As they swung away from the star the twigs on the base of the broom hit the star hard, spinning it towards Earth.

The Witch and Tom stopped the broom and looked on helplessly as the star fell to Earth then disappear as it hit the ground in a field of cows.

'OH NO! what have I done? The Universe can't survive missing a star!' the Witch cried.

'We need to recover the star and get it back into position.'

With that they zoomed off, chasing after the star hoping to find it and replace it in the sky before it was missed.

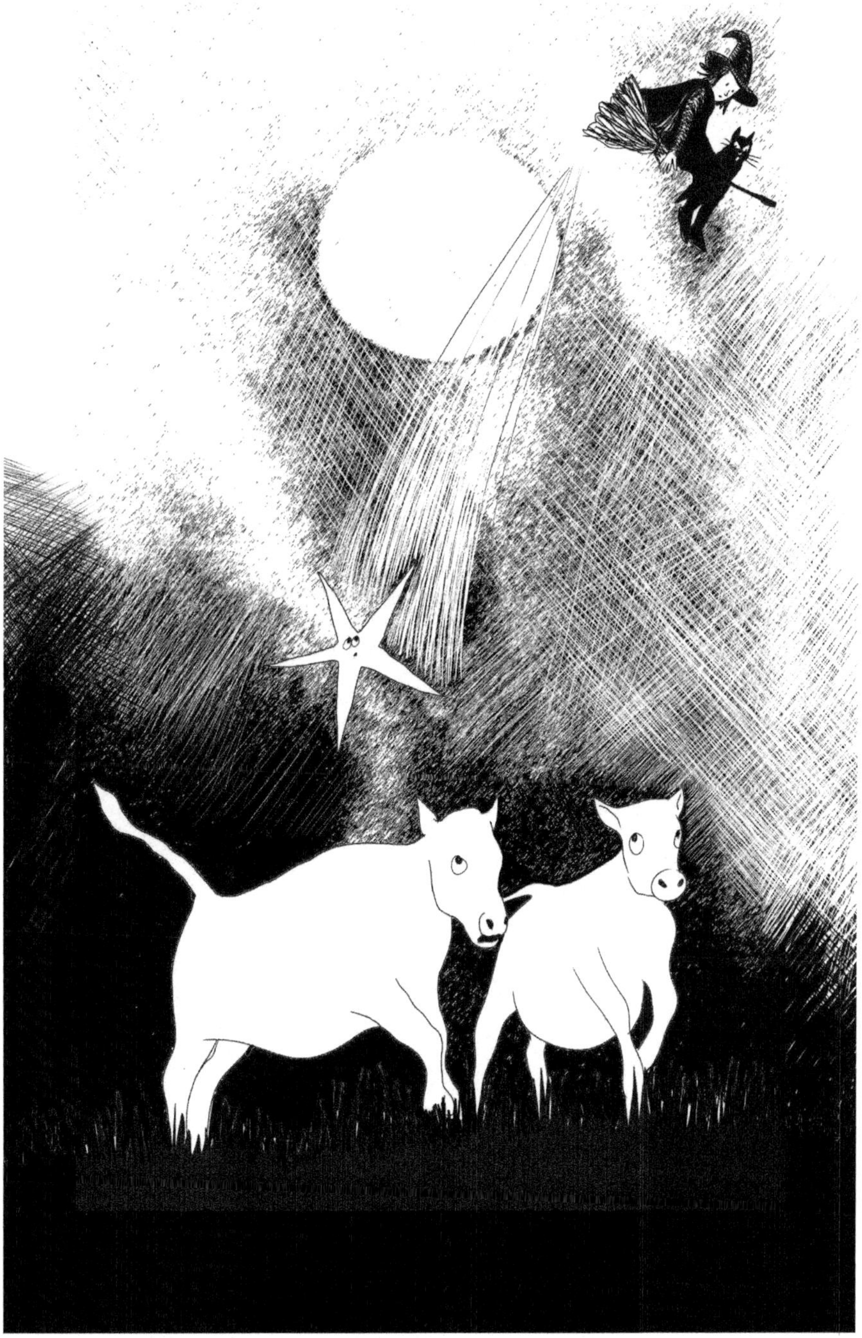

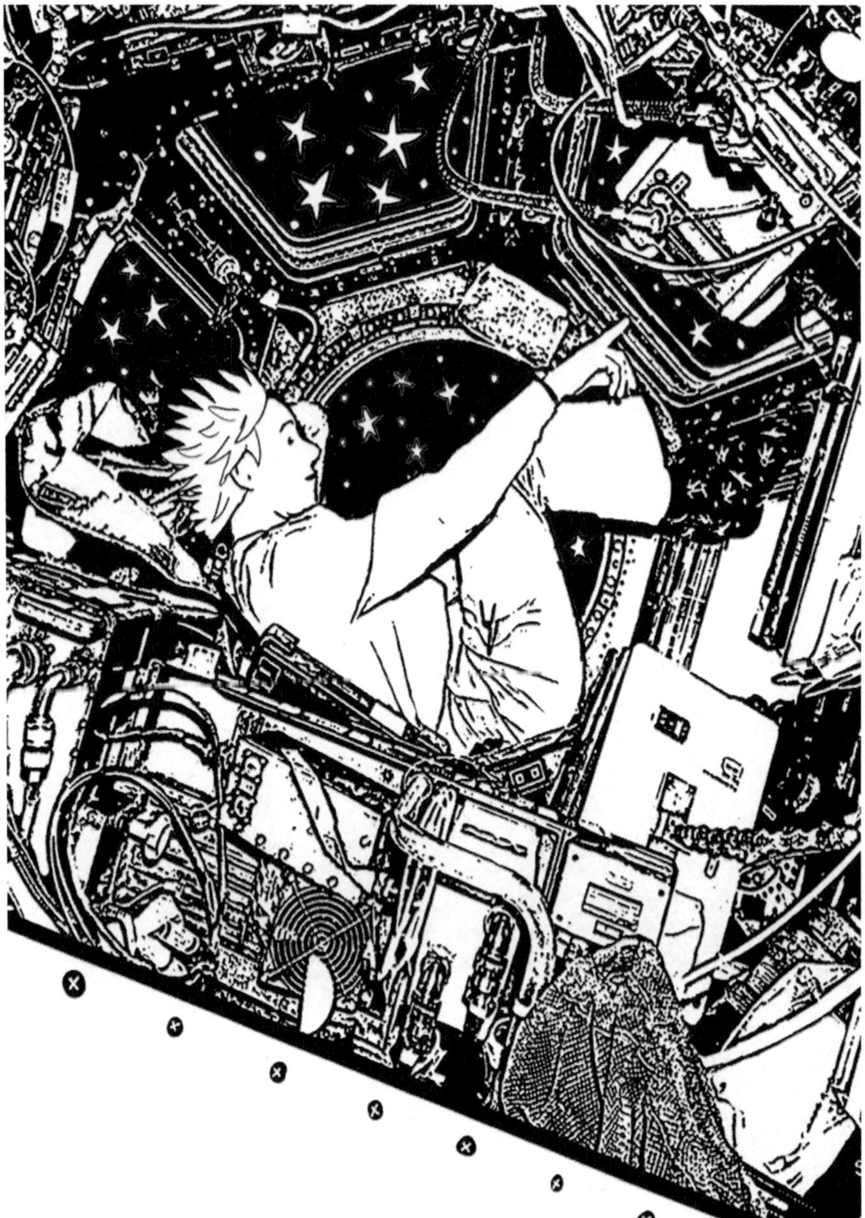

Across the other side of the world The International Space Station was in its orbit around the world, when the onboard computers picked up that a star was missing.

This triggered alarms and red flags on the computer screens which also sent alarms all around the World.

The astronauts flew weightlessly to their workstations to find out what had triggered the alarm. When they were strapped in their positions, they looked at the data with dismay. A star was missing. This was serious, what could cause a star to disappear? Could more stars disappear leaving an empty black sky?

They needed to find out what had happened.

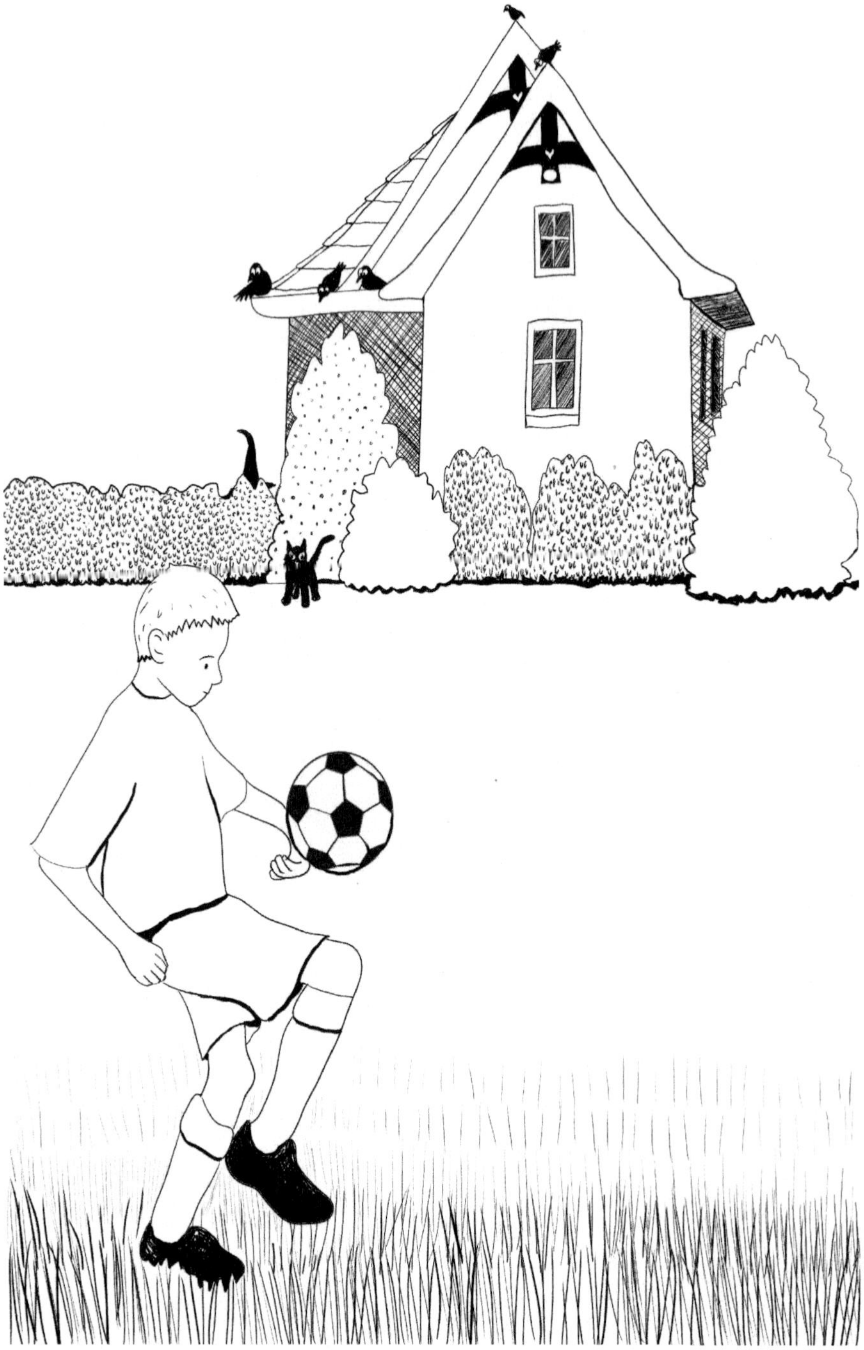

Meanwhile down on Earth, the Witch and Tom slowly flew over the field of cows where they thought the star had landed. After half an hour of flying backwards and forwards they decided they needed help. They would have to walk over the field slowly searching for the star.

They flew to Jack's house and landed behind the garden shed where no one would see them. As they landed, they saw Jack practising his football skills in the garden. Jack was practising keeping the ball in the air.

He was up to one hundred and twenty when he heard someone call his name.

'Jack! Jack! It's me the Witch.'

Jack dropped the ball then turned to look, there was the Witch and Tom peering round the back of the shed.

'What are you doing here? It's not that I'm not happy to see you, but what is it?' Jack asked.

The Witch quickly explained how she had knocked a star out of the sky with the broom, and she and Tom needed Jack's help to find it.

'Of course, I will, let's get on your broom, we're wasting time!' Jack replied.

They quickly jumped on the broom then flew to the field. The Witch quietly landed in the corner of the field beside a hedge not to frighten the cows.

They agreed to slowly walk up the field in straight lines a metre apart so they wouldn't miss anything.

Up and down they walked avoiding the cows and cow pats left on the ground.

They were becoming quite concerned when after an hour they hadn't found the star. Jack's back was getting sore from bending over. He went to step over the umpteenth smelly cow pat when looking at it something shone. He stopped and looked closer.

There faintly glimmering through the smelly mess was the star.

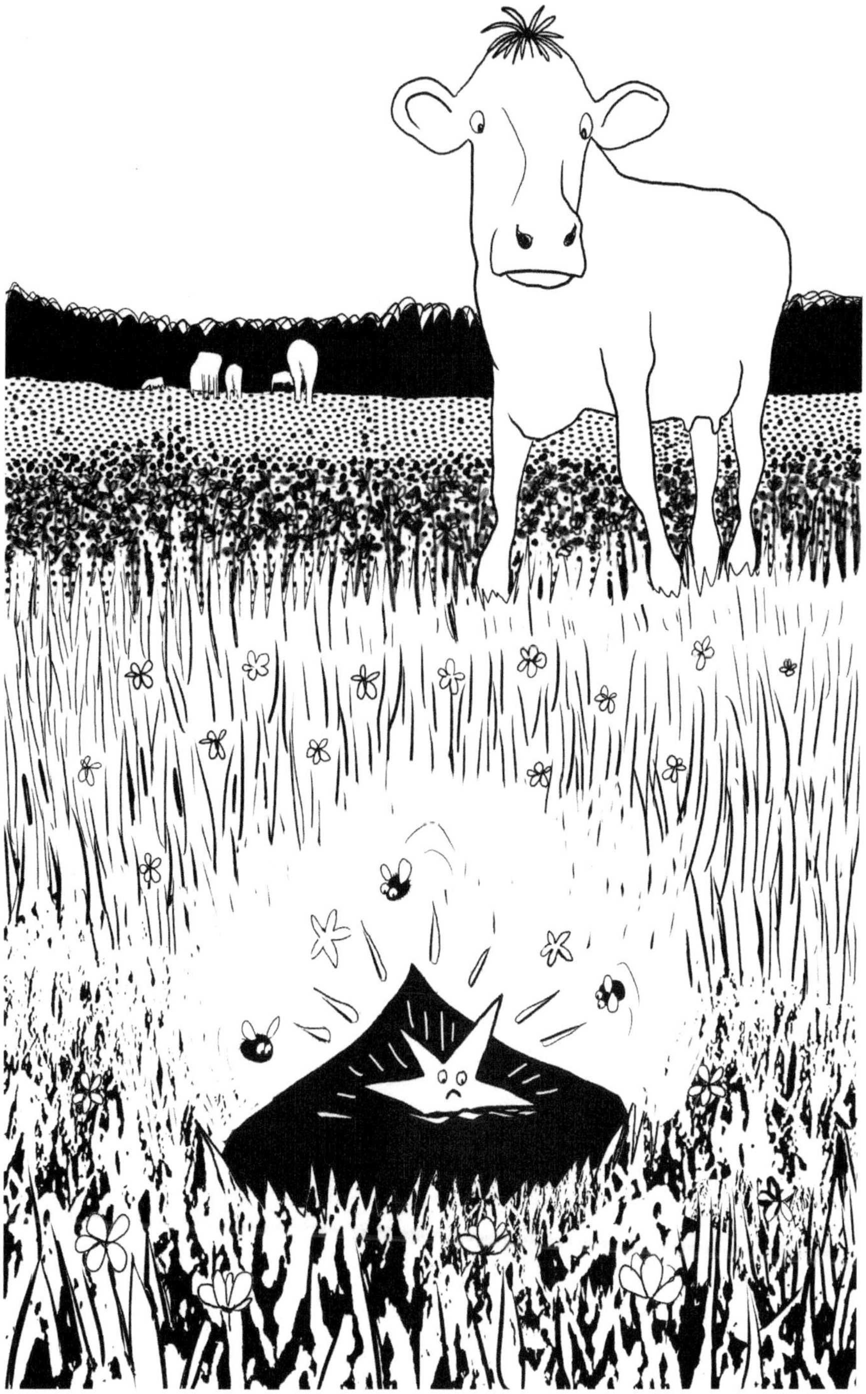

'Over here!' Jack shouted!

'I think I've found it. Look in the cow pat!'

The Witch and Tom rushed over. There it was, covered in green slimy cow mess, but it looked okay. They circled the cow pat holding their noses with their hands and paws, it was a fresh pat and it smelled. Tom and Jack turned away from the pat and looked at the Witch. She smiled.

'I get the message. I knocked it out of the sky so I should pull it out of the mess.'

Jack and Tom were holding their hands and paws over their noses because of the smell but nodded their heads up and down in agreement.

'Okay, here I go,' said the Witch.

She knelt, took a deep breath then turned her head away from the smell. She plunged her hands into the slimy green coloured pat and scooped up the star. She stood up holding the star away from her. It was smelly and had the cow poo running from it.

Jack and Tom looked on in amazement as the Witch took off and ran across the field. What they hadn't seen was a stream running down the side of the field which the Witch was heading towards. The cows scattered away from the Witch, startled by her rushing past.

The Witch reached the stream plunging her hands and the star into the water. After a few moments of washing, her hands and the star were clean.

She walked towards Jack and Tom with a smile holding the star which having been cleaned was shining brightly.

'Jack, thank you.' The Witch said, 'but we'll need to get going. It'll soon be dark. We need to get the star back in position before night. Can you walk home?'

'Of course,' Jack replied, 'I'll look for the star tonight. Go on. Get it back in the sky.'

The witch gave Jack a cuddle and Tom rubbed himself against Jack's legs, then they jumped onto the broom.

As they took off the Witch shouted to Jack, 'Look at the moon tonight.'

Then with a whoosh they were gone.

That night Jack looked at the moon from his bedroom window. It was a full moon and as he watched a silhouette of the Witch and Tom flew across it waving to Jack. He high fived back.

When they were out of sight he went to bed, dreaming about the next time they would meet.

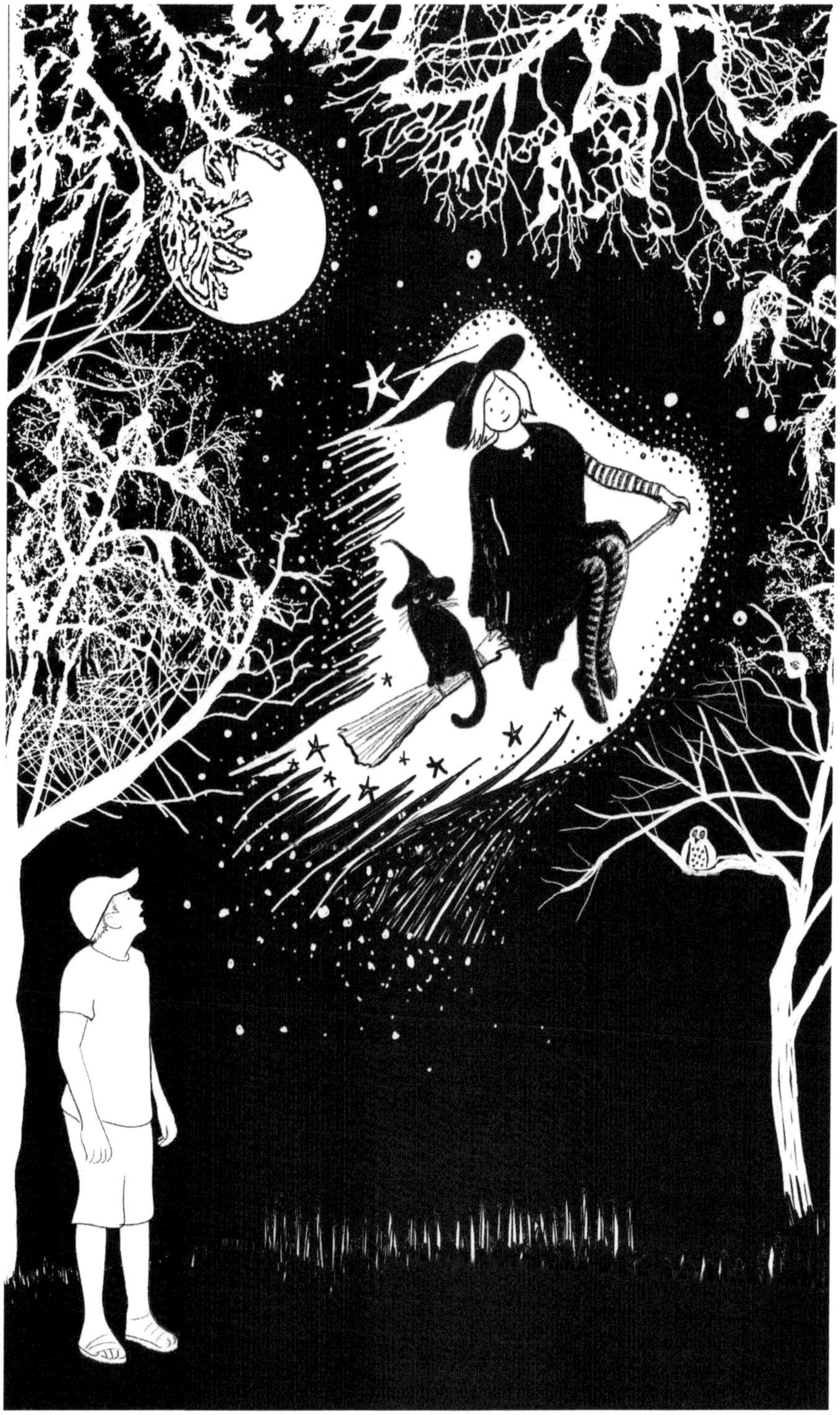

That night on The International Space Station the astronauts checked the stars and to their amazement they were all in the correct place. Had there been a fault in their systems? They were certain a star was missing last night, but stars cannot disappear then reappear. It wasn't logical, there had to be an explanation.

As one astronaut looked out to the stars and moon, she did a double take. She thought she saw a witch and a cat flying past on a broom. She shook her head closed her eyes then looked again. Nothing. it must have been an illusion, after all there are no such thing, as magic, fairies or witches on brooms, are there?

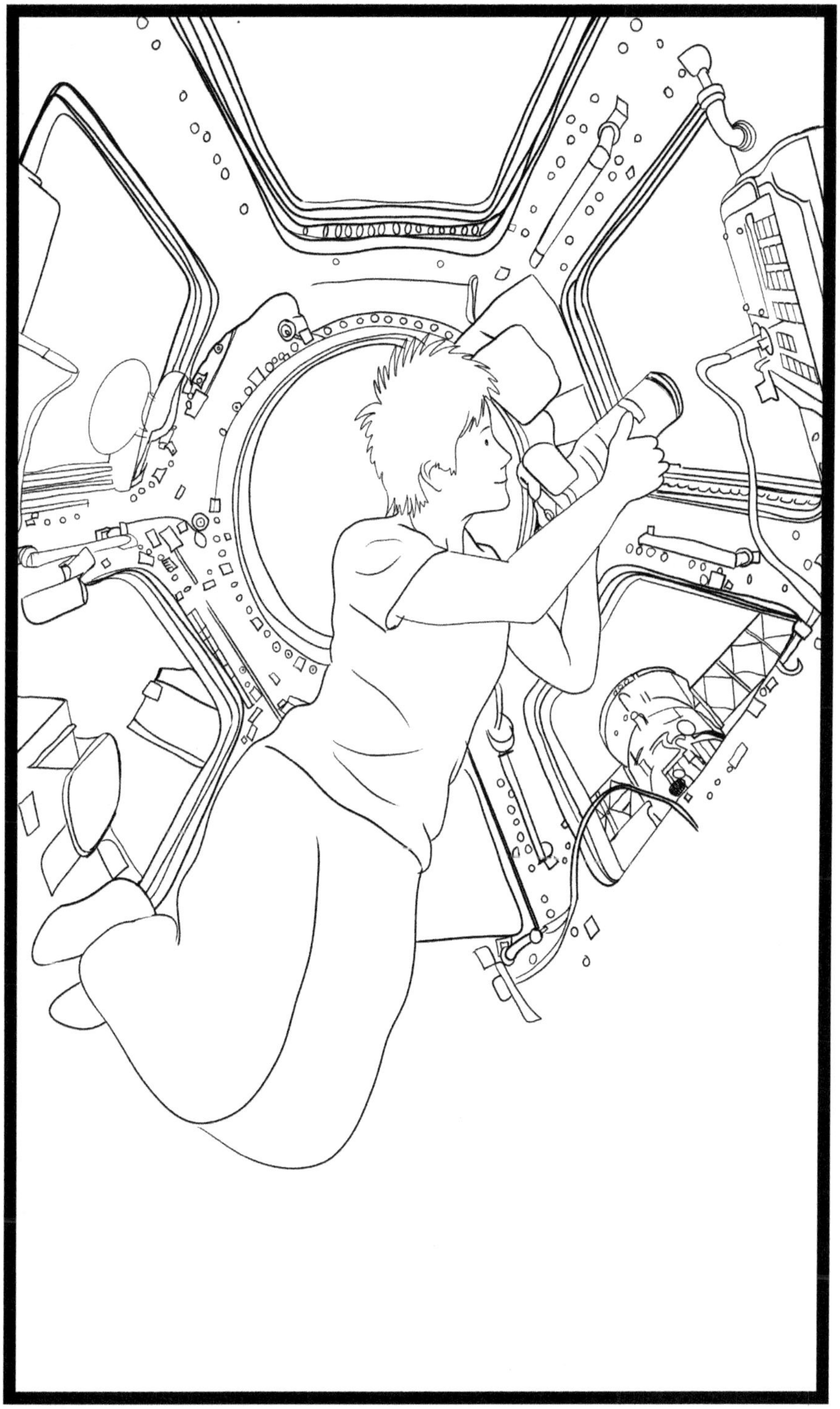

More Stories by Geoff Swift

The Friendly Giant Called Zak and
His Friend Rory the Misnamed
Monster

Rory Never Learns:
A Mediterranean Sea Adventure
With Zak and Rory

Zak and Rory's Toughest Journey:
With Zak and Rory

Brian the Beetroot's Haircut

Printed in Great Britain
by Amazon